UNFULFILLED

A HORROR LOVE STORY

ANNE PEARSON

STOCKWELL

PUBLISHERS SINCE 1898

Published in 2022 by
Anne Pearson
in association with
Arthur H Stockwell Ltd
West Wing Studios
Unit 166, The Mall
Luton, Bedfordshire
ahstockwell.co.uk

British Library Cataloguing-in-Publication Data:
A catalogue record for this book is
available from the British Library.
ISBN 9780722351390

About the Author

Anne Pearson was born in Lancaster where she lived for thirty-two years, after which she moved to Portsmouth where she has resided since 1962. Anne was a teacher of special needs children for thirty-seven years and says she learned much from them and considered it a privilege to have worked with these pupils. A widow with a daughter and two sons, Anne has been writing 'bits and pieces' all her life. *Unfulfilled* is her first 'real' book however, and mirrors certain events in her own life... although she has never committed murder, as far as she knows!

Chapter 1

I've been watching him for some time, the man across the road. Comes and goes, he does. I feel very sorry for him. It's his wife, you see – at least, I presume it's his wife! Terrible life she leads him, or so everybody says – everybody being his immediate neighbours as they are the ones who hear all the rows going on! Nobody seems to have actually seen his wife, but there's no doubt they've heard her shouting and screaming abuse at her poor husband.

She's some sort of invalid, I understand – never goes out. And that's odd because those who know a bit about her and her husband, well, they say there's nothing he wouldn't do to please her. Like I hear she loves daffodils and he took bunches and bunches of them in to her all through spring for as long as they were available. Yet you'd think he'd get her out for a change, in a wheelchair or a taxi or something. He hasn't got a car. I mean, they moved in three months ago. Funny her never going out of the house for three months. Can you imagine? I'd go mad. Still, maybe she doesn't ever want to go out. You never see any visitors going in there either.

But where was I? Oh yes, I was going to tell you about the man on the radio the other night. He set me thinking. Well, he was just like the man across the road from me in so far as he had an invalid wife too. They could be one and the same, right down to the daffodils – except on the radio they were roses. And that story had a very mysterious outcome!

I've only seen the man over the road to speak to twice. The first time was about four weeks ago when we were both at the bus stop. It wasn't more than a "Good morning" from each of us and a comment from me that I hoped he'd settled in happily in the area. He just smiled – rather wanly, I remember.

The second time was about two weeks ago, when I was walking a little distance behind him down my road, coming back from a bit of shopping. He'd dropped one of his parcels and I ran to pick it up for him. We both kind of rose from the pavement together and I was so close to him I thought we'd collide!

"Thank you so much. How very kind," he said – a clear, crisp sort of voice, full of promise.

I felt he'd have liked to have said more; he didn't – just sort of smiled at me resignedly and turned and went up the drive and into his house.

And that's when I actually heard her myself – his wife! The louvre windows were open at the top. Full throttle she was – a high-pitched screaming voice! She was giving him some stick, I can tell you. I slowed my pace a bit to hear what she was shouting about, but it was just a jumble of meaningless screeches. A crash of something followed, then total silence. I hurried indoors.

I could hear her shouting again tonight – more hysterics. I went out in the front garden in the pretence of chasing a dog which has been constantly fouling the flower beds; the dog was there all right, and I chased it off, but I really wanted to hear better what was going on over the road. I couldn't tell what she was shouting exactly, but from the tone it sounded awful.

You never hear him raise his voice – not once. He's so patient, that man. He had a large plaster across his forehead later when I saw him going out. I wondered if she had thrown something at him. You do hear of men and domestic violence, but not so often of women being the guilty ones – especially if the woman is an invalid! Supposedly, that is! There was an awful crash over the road a couple of days ago. A vase came flying through the open window – glass everywhere. He came out a bit later to clear up the mess.

Chapter 2

They all feel sorry for him round here – everybody's talking about them. They moved in about three months ago, as I said before. I don't think anyone actually witnessed the move. Mrs Jackson told me about it. She lives next door to them, and what Mrs Jackson doesn't know isn't worth knowing! So it is all the more unusual that she didn't see the moving-in going on. She doesn't miss a thing as a rule. The house opposite had been empty for over six months, ever since poor old Mr Olsen died. He was found dead in there by the postman – been dead for over a week and nobody knew! They did say he'd never got over his wife disappearing a year before that. She went out one morning to get her shopping as usual and she hasn't been seen or heard of from that day to this! The police are still investigating, of course, but what happened to her or where she is . . . well, it's as great a mystery as ever it was. They had to have a post-mortem on Mr Olsen to establish how he died. It said in the paper 'natural causes', but Mrs Jackson said she knew different, whatever that might mean. But she would say that, wouldn't she?

Next thing the house was up for sale. An estate agent's board was soon to be seen in the front garden advertising the property. He didn't seem to have any relatives – Mr Olsen, that is. I only heard of two lots of people viewing the property when it was up for sale, and neither party came back. Mind you, the place was a bit run-down, needed updating and repair and it had never had a lick of paint on the outside for as long as I can remember and I've lived here for over nine years. That's why everybody round here was surprised to see it occupied all of a sudden three months ago. Mrs Jackson knocked at the door to introduce herself right away, but the new owner didn't invite her in. He was polite but non-committal, she told me.

She said she knocked to see if they needed any help, but we all know she was just being nosey as usual! Anyway, she met her match this time – he wasn't having any. He kept her firmly at bay! She didn't like this kind of thing at all, so she comforted herself ever after by gossiping to all and sundry about even the smallest snippets she could learn about her new neighbours. It was usually derogatory, as you can imagine.

Chapter 3

Good heavens, is that the time? I'm late for Jim's meal. He's usually eaten and all cleared away by now. I must be slipping! I'd better get a move on. Oh, my name's Martha, by the way. Didn't I say? Sorry. We all had biblical names in our family – my father insisted on that. Well, he would, being a vicar, wouldn't he? He always saw that certain Christian principles were adhered to, and seeing we all had names from the Bible was one of them. My father was Jacob, my mother was Sara, and my sister was Ruth and my brother Aaron. Sadly we lost Aaron in a train crash ten years ago. And, as you know, there's me – Martha.

But I digress. It's high time I saw to Jim. I suppose in a way I'm in the same situation as the man across the road. He's got her, his invalid wife, to see to and I've got Jim to look after. Come to think of it, Jim never goes out ever, just like her across from me, but then that's Jim's choice. He can't go out, really. You see, his mind's gone – most of the time, anyway. Not that he's often violent or anything like that, you understand, but he has this phobia: he's terrified of leaving his room upstairs. Sometimes he even believes he can't walk! But as long as he remains in his room he's more or less all right. I used to try to get him downstairs, but he got so distressed I gave up and he hasn't bothered since. Leave well alone, as my mother used to say. She was right. Jim likes to be in his room on his own most of the time, but I do always insist on spending at least one hour every evening with him from nine till ten and that's sacrosanct – even

Mrs Jackson observes that one. She gets curious sometimes as she's never set eyes on him – not even once! But that's Jim's wish; and if he can't have his own way in that . . . well, there isn't much else he ever asks for.

I expect you're wondering how all this came about. Well, I'll tell you. Jim and I were to have been married some ten years ago on June the 10th 1952. The sad thing was my mother and father would not be there to witness it, for Mother died the preceding January and Father followed her in the March. Jim attended my father's church and he had taken to walking me home after the Sunday evening service. After this we met regularly, and six months later Jim asked me to marry him. I said yes, and the wedding was planned.

Little did I know what lay ahead! Just one week before the wedding something went very wrong with Jim's brain and it was all off – no marriage, no nothing! Jim didn't even know who I was. You can imagine the state all this left me in. I don't think Jim realises who I am now either. He calls me Maggie sometimes instead of my own name, Martha. I found out a little while ago, when I found some old letters Jim had kept, that he was once engaged to a girl called Maggie before he met me. Still, it doesn't make much difference now, does it? I mean, I'm not jealous. How could you be jealous about somebody who doesn't remember he once loved you and was going to be your husband? No, it's no good worrying about that kind of thing any more.

I've a lot to be thankful for though. I've got my health and I've got my books. I get through two or three a week from our local library – mostly love stories. They remind me of what I never had, I suppose! And of course I've got Jim – not the Jim I once knew, I know, but the fact is that if I didn't see to him he'd have been in a mental home for the rest of his life and I wasn't having that! I felt I owed him that at least.

When I look back to when we were courting I can recall occasions when I noticed Jim acting rather oddly. It was his moods. Usually he was fine, but sometimes he'd go so morose and into himself it could be a bit frightening and I could never work out what caused it. Still, I never used to take much notice and sooner or later he was back to normal again.

He could fashion just about anything given wood and the tools. He had several interesting hobbies too. He bred budgerigars, he did his own wine-making and he belonged to two amateur dramatic societies. I was in one of Jim's drama groups, but all that changed with the happenings on Jim's stag night.

He had decided to have his night out well before the wedding so as to be at his best on 'the day'. He always used to talk about some of his friends who'd had stag nights the very night before their weddings, and they'd hardly been sober enough next day to realise it was the 'big day'.

The stag night had started well enough, evidently, but towards the end of the evening, when they reached their eighth pub, an argument broke out between Jim and Bernard. Bernard was to be Jim's best man. Things went from bad to worse, the effects of alcohol adding fuel to the fire, so to speak! Quite out of character, they'd lashed out at one another and the rest of the party had hustled them out of the pub and made tracks for home before the police were called – the landlord had threatened such action.

Five of the party, including Jim and Bernard, went in the direction of the railway bridge. What happened next was never quite clear, except that some stupidity went on on top of the bridge parapet, between Jim and Bernard. They both climbed up there, evidently, which was no mean feat at the best of times. But if you'd had a drop too much to drink – well! A railway worker found a dead body between the tracks on the up line, just by the bridge, a little while afterwards. The body was later identified as that of Bernard Evans, Jim's best-man-to-be! At the inquest, sometime after, Jim acted very strangely, just muttering incoherently, as he does now often. During his jumbled speech Jim seemed to suggest that Bernard fell off the bridge accidentally, but two witnesses who came forward were almost certain that Jim had pushed him! The others accompanying Jim and Bernard home that night said they couldn't be certain what happened, but they testified that Jim was in a very wild state of mind.

The marriage was off indefinitely after that. Perhaps it was a case of 'diminished responsibility', but there was a 'lack of real evidence' and the verdict was 'not guilty'. Nevertheless the court insisted Jim was to be examined by a psychiatrist appointed by a judge. Jim was subjected to a searching examination, both physical and mental, with endless tests. The result was that Jim was declared insane and potentially dangerous to himself and to others. He was to be secured in a mental institution for the rest of his life! Well, you can imagine what that did to me, just about to be married! Not that Jim's affair and mine had been a mad, passionate one or anything like that, but we'd known one another a while and it had developed into a happy enough companionship so we'd decided to marry. I knew, as I said before, that Jim had a few odd ways, but I certainly never anticipated anything like this happening just before our wedding. It was a terrible blow! After the initial shock of it all, one thing began to stand out clearly in my mind. It was this: on no account, I decided, was my Jim going to spend the rest of his days in a mental home! I didn't know how I would prevent it exactly, but I determined I'd beat the system somehow. And I did, but I'll let you into that little secret a bit later on.

Chapter 4

It's his birthday tomorrow. I always get him a card and a present. I bought him a budgie yesterday – a lovely blue shade, with paler-blue tail feathers. I've got a suitable cage indoors, so I only had to buy the seed, new feeding pots, the sanded paper to put in the bottom of the cage, plus a few 'bird' toys. I think I mentioned that Jim used to breed budgerigars himself when he was younger, so I thought that this might possibly revive a few happy memories for him. The budgie should be a bit of company for him, I thought, though he doesn't seem to need any. Very strange! Anyway, he shall have the bird tomorrow and we'll see if he likes it or not. If he doesn't, I'll have it myself and keep it downstairs. You can only try, can't you?

My sister Ruth was quite funny about Jim and me at first – you know, about us living together when we weren't married. But, as I told her, it was never going to be that kind of living together, was it? Well, not with Jim in his state of mind. I think he looks on me as more of a sister really. And as for our courtship, well, you'd think it had never taken place so far as Jim is concerned. They do say that what you've never had you never miss. It was like that for Jim and me, but I've learned to cope. It's been a bit like a bereavement, I suppose. Time is a great healer.

Funny, but I never think about men in that way now – well, at least, I didn't until I started noticing the man who moved in across the road from me. And now I'm not sure any more. I have this desire to help him in some way. I think it's because he seems so inoffensive and that wife of his treats him so dreadfully. She ought to be grateful she's got a husband who sees to her every need instead of railing at him constantly. He can hardly be happy over there with his wife screaming abuse at him most of the time. He looks quite sad on occasions, as if life has passed him by.

I've just remembered: I've left Jim's shirts on the line. They'll be dry now and it looks like rain. Back in a moment. That's better – only just in time too. The heavens are opening. The forecast said rain, and it was right for once. I usually iron straight away, but I feel a bit tired tonight so I'll do them in the morning. I think I'll make a drink for Jim and I'll have an early night.

Chapter 5

"Oh, please come in," I said.

It was the man from across the road.

"Thank you," he said as he stepped into the hallway. "I am so sorry to trouble you at this early hour of the day, but I saw you were about. It's my wife, you see. You probably know she's confined to a wheelchair. Well, somehow she slipped out of her chair and fell awkwardly; she appears to have twisted her ankle and it's swelled up quite badly. She is in considerable pain, I'm afraid. A cold-water bandage would help, and I wondered if you possibly have such a thing?" he asked.

"Of course – I've plenty of that sort of thing. No trouble at all. I'll just go and get some for you," I told him.

I went into the lounge. He followed me tentatively. I felt his eyes observing all the details of the room as I looked out the crêpe bandages.

I turned to him and said, "But shouldn't you be sending for the doctor in the circumstances, or would I be of any help if I came over?"

His face stiffened visibly as he replied, "Oh no, indeed – no need for a doctor or you. Forgive me – I don't wish to appear rude or ungrateful. It's just that my wife never sees anyone – except me that is. She's funny that way, you know." He seemed very embarrassed.

I handed him the bandages.

"There you are. There are two different widths, I do hope they'll be helpful."

11

"Thank you. Oh, thank you so much – so very kind of you," he said. "I'll replace them, of course. It's just that the chemist isn't open yet or I shouldn't have troubled you and I wanted to help my wife as soon as possible," he said almost apologetically.

"Oh, don't worry about replacements – I've plenty. Only too pleased to help any time, and if you need anything else . . . " I said.

I replaced the first-aid box in the cupboard and turned round, but he was gone! He'd gone quite suddenly. I was just in time to see him disappear through his front door as I looked across the road! I felt somewhat angry at first and bewildered at the suddenness of his departure, but then I realised that he probably thought he'd said too much about his wife and so on. After all, he did keep himself to himself. There's one thing for certain: he'd never have gone to Mrs Jackson for help, I know. She is far too inquisitive.

I felt quite glad then that it was me he had asked for help. What was more, I had that peculiar feeling again. It was a bit like just before you go on stage to say your lines. Not that I ever had many lines to say at our drama presentations! Jim was the star. I remember Jim had the lead years ago in *Salad Days* and I was just an extra in the crowd. What was it about my neighbour across the road that disturbed me so? It was certainly different from anything I'd ever experienced before, I knew.

Oh, there's the doorbell again. . . . It was Mrs Jackson. She only wanted to know about Clive and what he came over to my house for. She doesn't miss much, I can tell you.

"Yes, Clive – that's his name," she told me. "Didn't you know?"

"No, I didn't," I said. I told Mrs Jackson about the bandage business.

"Well, I think there's something really weird going on next door to me," she said. "The rows, the noise – it's simply dreadful. If she's supposed to be such an invalid I don't know how she has the energy to cause such a riot. And, you know, she never has anyone going to see her – except Clive, of course. Mind you, who'd want to visit her? I wonder."

And then she was gone – same as usual. I never really knew what she came for – just a gossip, I expect. At least I've got to know the name of my neighbour opposite: Clive, eh? I haven't known any man with that particular name before. It just struck me that it wasn't a name my father would have approved of! Jim got away with it, being a James originally. My father insisted we all had biblical names, as I told you before. My mother wanted to call me Deirdre, but my father soon put a stop to that. He called me Martha, whether she liked it or not.

Chapter 6

I'll have to answer my sister's letter, I suppose. She wants to come and stay here, but she can't and that's that. It's Jim, you see – won't have her near the place, or anybody else for that matter. He blames her, in his more lucid moments, for the way he is. Not that he remembers he was once to be married years ago or anything, but he knows something went very wrong and he seems to think my sister was responsible. The trouble is he thinks she's his sister! He hasn't even got a sister. But I just go along with what he thinks – he's happier that way. If my sister, Ruth, can't come here, then I know she'd like me to stay with her for a change. She says it would do me good. Well, I dare say it would, but how can I leave Jim?

"Put him in a home for a couple of weeks," she says. That won't happen. I'll explain later why that is not possible.

My sister lives on her own. She was only married a few months when her husband was killed in a train accident. A bit of a coincidence that, with my brother, Aaron, dying in a train crash too, don't you think? We don't seem to have been very fortunate in our family so far, do we? But I look at it this way: when something tragic happens in your life it probably lets you out of something even worse which could have occurred. Thinking that way, I don't feel so bad about everything. I always say don't expect anything to go right, then you can't be disappointed. And if things go well it's a bonus!

I don't worry too much about not being able to go away when I want. I'm used to Jim and our way of life now, and he's company of a kind as well. It's Jim's birthday today. I've made him a cake, so I hope he'll like it. Half the time he doesn't understand what it means, but it may just please him. He's fifty-six today. He's ten years older than me. It's quite uncanny how the number ten features in our lives. Like Jim's ten years older than me; we were to have been married on the 10th and it would have been our tenth wedding anniversary in May gone. Oh, and we live at number ten. And its Jim's birthday today – the 10th!

As you can gather, neither of us were spring chickens when we were to marry. I remember Jim saying we'd better be quick or we'd miss it – well, we did, didn't we? It's strange how things have turned out, but you can get used to anything if you try hard enough.

He's been a bit down tonight – Jim, I mean. I can always tell because he's gone off his food. I made him a lovely ham salad. It had just about everything in it, but it came downstairs the same way it went up – untouched. His chocolate ice cream was all melted too. Normally that's his favourite – asks for more, in fact. Never mind – perhaps he'll feel better tomorrow.

He's getting more difficult to live with too. He has these black moods when he kind of growls when I go in to him or else he just sits there, staring into space and slavering down one side of his mouth. He never used to do that.

When I told Mrs Jackson about it, she said was I sure he wouldn't harm me? She said I might not be safe with him in the house and he'd be best 'put away'. I've never told Mrs Jackson the truth about Jim and me – the less anyone knows in the circumstances the better. I nearly exploded at Mrs Jackson's suggestion about Jim, I can tell you! Poor Jim – he can't help it.

He's started another peculiar habit lately too. He talks to an imaginary 'friend' in his room. He just looks across at the empty chair in the opposite corner of the room and carries on a conversation! When you've listened for a while you'd swear there really was somebody there he was talking to. I almost got to believing it myself last night, Jim was so convincing. Maybe that's the actor bit of years ago in Jim coming out again. He could almost be awarded an Oscar for his latest performance. That's what small children do sometimes when they're playing, don't they? They invent an imaginary friend to talk to – especially a child who is the only one in the family. I read about it somewhere. Maybe Jim is going back to his childhood – the Seven Ages of Man, and all that!

I wonder sometimes what would happen to Jim if I was taken seriously ill or something. Who'd look after him? If one of us has to die, then I just pray he goes first.

Jim's made his own coffin upstairs in the spare room and it's ready for when it's needed, so Jim says! Beautiful job he's made of it too – all brass handles and real oak. None of your cheap veneer and plastic trimmings. It took him a long time, mind. I expect it wasn't too difficult for him, though, seeing as he used to be a master carpenter. I used to go to furniture sales and bring Jim old oak chests of drawers back and suchlike. He dismantled them, cut pieces to the sizes he needed, rubbed them down, stained and polished them; and then he'd assemble the whole lot to the design required. He wouldn't have any factory-made glue either; he made it himself using bones I'd bring him from the butcher. Sometimes there'd be an awful stink all over the house from the glue-making! Jim still has all his carpentry tools in the spare room and a gas ring for making his glue. I really got it for him to make a drink when he fancied one. So long as he doesn't set the place on fire! I do worry about the possibility. It took Jim months to complete his coffin. I was a bit upset when I saw he'd used my wedding dress and some silk to pad out all the inside of the coffin. Jim must have found my wedding dress in the cupboard at the top of the stairs and decided that was what he needed! Well, it would have been my wedding dress if there'd ever been a wedding! I suppose I kept it for sentimental reasons. I am glad I kept it in good order – at least it's ended up serving some useful purpose. Jim's put sprigs of lavender in the coffin to keep it smelling sweet.

Chapter 7

I promised you a bit ago I'd let you into my little secret about how I managed to save Jim from spending the rest of his life in a mental institution. Well, here's how it came about. You'll remember that after the tragedy of the stag night and the death of Bernard Jim was certified insane and was to be confined to a mental home for life. I pleaded with Jim's doctor to prevent this happening, but to no avail. I tried one more time. I saw a different doctor – someone new. The first of Jim's doctors was evidently away on a three-month course, and this new young doctor was taking his place till his return. I explained at length to this new doctor that he must help prevent Jim going into mental care. I felt desperate and determined that, whatever it took, I'd keep Jim with me. I know what you're thinking: I must have been mad! Well, maybe I was! Emotions are strange things – dangerous things at times! In a rash moment I did a terrible thing. I told the doctor if he would help me achieve what I wanted, he'd be compensated handsomely.

Money was no problem for me as I had recently been left a rather large legacy quite out of the blue! The money was left to me by an old parishioner who had attended my late father's church for years. Her name was Mrs Morton. In my early twenties I used to help Mrs Morton with her shopping and other bits and pieces as she became housebound. We became very good friends, but I lost touch with her over the years. That's why I was so surprised when a letter came for me from Mrs Morton's solicitor, informing me of the legacy. It was such a large sum! To say I was flabbergasted would be an understatement! It seems Mrs Morton had no living relatives, so she had decided to leave her money in my favour. I knew that with my good fortune I would have no financial worries for the rest of my life.

I knew that what I had asked the doctor was wrong, but I didn't care. It was an age before he spoke. At first the doctor said he could not help me, but as the monetary offer rose he changed his mind somewhat. He told me to leave him to think about it and he would contact me later. And this he did. We had several meetings the next week. At this time Jim was in the psychiatric unit of the hospital where my doctor friend worked. For your benefit we'll call the doctor Dr Smith, though that is not his real name. Jim was on Dr Smith's list along with other patients, and Jim was seen by him daily. Jim's stay at this unit was only to be temporary as he would be in a mental institution for life shortly.

Dr Smith was going to help me, though I didn't know how he was going to achieve it. I was aware that what I was asking was unlawful and it would be the same for Dr Smith if we should be found out! Evidently the temptation of considerable gain outweighed Dr Smith's honouring his Hippocratic oath! Jim was all that concerned me. I duly gave Dr Smith a large cheque and he started the ball rolling.

The plan was that the 'death' of Jim should be arranged – not the real thing, of course! Dr Smith did his daily rounds of his patients. All went well at first, but on Dr Smith's third visit round the ward Jim was found to be unconscious and he 'died' a few minutes later. He had been given a special injection by Dr Smith which gave the appearance of Jim being dead. As the death was sudden a second opinion was necessary, so another doctor was called to verify the cause of death. This is common practice in such circumstances. Let's call this second doctor Dr Jones. This is, of course, not his real name. You may be thinking there could be a problem regarding this second opinion, but you needn't worry. And why not? I am about to tell you. Dr Jones was a great friend of Dr Smith, and Dr Smith persuaded Dr Jones to join him in carrying out my wishes – especially as he saw the chance of good remuneration. The plot thickens, as you might say!

I didn't care what they did so long as I got Jim back with me. That afternoon Jim's 'death' was indeed certified, 'heart failure' being entered on the death certificate. In due course I had the death certificate in my hand and the doctors had cheques from me in theirs! All parties seemed well satisfied with the exchanges. But of course it wasn't Jim in the coffin; it was Jim's body weight in sand!

Next the 'funeral' had to be arranged. It was fortunate the funeral was arranged quickly – just three days after Jim's 'death'. Somehow the doctors had managed to keep Jim 'dead' until he was brought home to me. They then arranged the funeral and everything for me. Dr Smith and Dr Jones, meanwhile, contacted an undertaker friend of theirs and drew him into their web of deceit, getting him to provide a coffin and the necessary paperwork – forged, of course! And that was Jim awaiting his burial as far as the hospital was concerned.

The doctors evidently paid the undertaker quite well for his 'services'! It crossed my mind that this was probably not the first time these three had colluded in questionable practices!

There were only four at the graveside. They were two of Jim's friends from the infamous stag night, my sister, Ruth, and me. Jim had few relatives except for a couple of nephews living in Australia – hence the small number of us at the funeral, which was all to the good in the circumstances. The funeral passed off well enough, but of course it wasn't Jim in the casket, was it? I couldn't bring myself to shed any tears at the graveside. Jim's friends thought this was on account of my being in too great a state of shock! And that wasn't far from the truth.

We dispersed after the burial, and that was Jim gone as far as Jim's friends were concerned. Only my sister, Ruth, knew of my dreadful secret. We'd always been very close and shared everything when we were young. The fact that we saw little of each other nowadays wasn't going to alter anything. I knew I could trust her implicitly. The next thing for me to do was to move to another part of the country, where nobody knew us. Safer that way, I thought.

I had one more meeting with Dr Smith and Dr Jones. We were to keep in touch for if and when I needed them, with the usual reward arrangements in operation. Before I moved, Dr Smith came to my house and he gave Jim an injection which brought Jim out of his comatose state and back to reality.

So it was that I came to live at my present address with Jim living upstairs in his room. It was his wish to be up there. He positively shook when I asked him if he'd like a room downstairs, but I don't know the reason for that.

I think it's been worthwhile what I did for Jim, anyway. Though observing him lately I wonder if he's long for this world. I've noticed one or two changes in Jim's behaviour. Like he's just finished etching his name on a brass plate – ready to be fixed on the coffin lid at a later date, I suppose. It reads:

R.I.P.
JAMES EDWARD MADDOX
DIED . . .
AGED . . .

He can hardly fill in the date of his death or the age at which he died, now, can he? It's a lovely brass plate he's done his engraving on. I got it in some sale I went to for him. Maybe this year's birthday will be his last.

Chapter 8

I was down at the market today. It was a nice bright day for a change and quite warm. I usually go there once a week as the fruit and vegetables are so much cheaper than elsewhere.

I'd bought a bit more than usual and I was having some difficulty managing so many bags when I heard a voice behind me say, "Allow me."

It was Clive!

"Oh, er, thank you, but I think I can manage," I stuttered.

"No, no, that lot is far too bulky and awkward. Here – let me. I'll take these two for you," he said politely but firmly. "After all, I've only one or two items of my own to carry and I imagine we'll both be going home in the same direction, eh?"

He was almost laughing by this time. It did me good to see it, he looked so melancholy usually.

"Well, if you're sure it's no trouble . . ." I began.

"Not a bit," he said. "I usually get a cup of coffee when I'm down here at the café over the way there. Would you care to join me?"

"That sounds like rather a good idea, and I'm in no great rush this morning," I said.

We had tea, in fact, and some of their famous buttered scones. It wasn't long before we were chatting easily about this and that. He proved an interesting talker and an even better listener. I couldn't help comparing him with Mrs Jackson, who was a very voluble talker yet she never had time – or inclination, it seemed to me – to listen to the other person. We finished our tea and I got up to go, but before I could stop him Clive had paid the bill.

"Oh, you shouldn't have done that. Please let me . . ." I began; but he interrupted me quickly, saying he wouldn't hear of such a thing. My paying my share of the bill, he meant. After all, he said, it was he who had suggested going for a drink. I promised I'd 'get him' next time.

"I'll look forward to that very much indeed," he said.

We both went home on the bus together; the chat was very general. He seemed to make a point of avoiding mentioning his wife or his own affairs, so I didn't pursue anything. We got off the bus at our stop and walked down the road. Clive helped me with my parcels to my front door and said he hoped we'd bump into each other again soon, and I said I hoped so too. Then he went over the road and up the drive to his house.

It didn't take two minutes before I heard his wife's strident tones coming through the open window. The row went on for about five minutes, then stopped. I wondered what on earth she'd found fault with this time. Whatever would it take to please that woman? I wondered.

I came across Clive quite often in the next few days, one way or another, and we became really friendly. He usually had a snippet to tell me which made me laugh. I enjoyed his company and began to look for opportunities to see him and talk. Somehow he added a new dimension to my life! It certainly made a change from being with Jim. I mean, I know Jim can't help the way he is, but you'd hardly call him good company. I knew too, in my heart, that Clive was beginning to mean something very special to me – very special indeed!

Chapter 9

It must be six months now since Clive and his wife moved in across the road from me. I feel as if I've known Clive a very long time – though his wife doesn't seem any better towards him, I'm sad to say. Last night in particular was a real humdinger! She really went for him. I could hear her as I put the milk bottles out. They always seem to leave their louvre windows open; otherwise we would not hear half so much as we do. The row went on for at least a quarter of an hour, then complete silence. I expect she's exhausted herself – and Clive!

Oh, look! There's a police car across the road right outside Clive's house. I wonder what's going on. I can see Mrs Jackson's net curtains twitching – she'll know all about it, I suppose. What she can't hear she can lip-read – it comes from years of practice. Oh dear! They're bringing Clive out of his house. He looks quite ill. He's actually getting into the police car! Well, would you believe it? There's one policeman left standing at Clive's front door, sort of guarding it. It looks quite ominous! I thought she couldn't resist it: there's Mrs Jackson just popped her head out of her front door and now she's pretending to look surprised at seeing a PC outside Clive's house. Good Lord! She's talking to him now – trust her! I expect she'll be over here shortly to tell me what she knows. She can never keep anything to herself.

It's over twelve hours now since Clive went off with the police. I mean, whatever can they want him for? And how's his wife managing by herself? That's what's bothering me. Maybe he's got someone in to look after her, though I can't say I've ever seen anyone going in there and I've been keeping an eye open for developments. You'll be thinking I'm getting as bad as Mrs Jackson if I go on like this, won't you? No, it's just that I feel a bit concerned about it all.

It's certainly been very quiet in the direction of Clive's house since he left. We've not had any of the usual hysterical outbursts. Still, if she's in there on her own there'll be no one to shout at, will there? The thing that's bothering me is this: whatever trouble can Clive be in for him to have gone off with the police? I do wonder! I'm very surprised that Mrs Jackson hasn't been over to me. She'll no doubt arrive soon with the latest news on the situation. She's bound to know something. Not that I think for one moment Clive would have asked her to look in on his wife. If he had done, she'd have a great old mooch around, I can tell you. I told Jim about the police being over the road, but he said we should mind our own business and keep ourselves to ourselves. Well, he observes that one, I'll grant him that. Must have had one of his lucid moments there, telling me all that.

Chapter 10

Still no sign of Clive, and it's the second day he's been gone. What can have happened? I've had a letter this morning. It was a sort of package – quite bulky, in fact. I couldn't make out the postmark. It was all blurred. The envelope was damp too. Must have been from the downpour we had early this morning. I opened the envelope, which wasn't difficult as all the 'sticky' had worn off with the rain. I took out the wodge of paper and started to read. It was neatly written, though a bit shaky in parts, as if the person writing had bad nerves.

It was indeed a letter from Clive. He began by explaining that the police had called on him to inform him of the death of his brother in a road accident. He had had to accompany them to identify that it was indeed his brother. Sad to say, it *was* Clive's brother and Clive had to stay on in the area to sort his brother's affairs out. But what followed in the letter gave me the greatest shock of my life!

Little did I know what I was about to read. There were over twelve pages! I just stared at the words. I must have gone over it at least ten times before I could accept, even to the smallest degree, what was written there! As to what followed, I was in a daze – shocked, bewildered and disbelieving! I had to sit down. I felt quite faint. Clive hadn't told me everything, he said, but enough for me to realise what a desperate situation he was in! I tried hard to disbelieve what I had read. It was unreal and shocking, and yet it must be true, horrific as it was. I was the one Clive was appealing to for help. I might have been flattered if things hadn't been so serious. Well, you can't get much more serious than dead, and that was what she was – DEAD – Clive's wife!

He said he'd never meant to kill her, but it had happened. I'm finding all this so hard to take in. I find it impossible to believe that Clive – such a gentle, tolerant man – has committed murder! For that was what it is: murder! This is the account which Clive wrote in his letter of what happened in his house on that fateful evening. Please read it for yourselves. Clive wrote:

How did I ever come to commit such a dreadful crime, Martha? I never meant to kill Esther, as God is my Judge, but I did. I have no excuses except that it had been one of those evenings when Esther shouted and belittled me from the security of her wheelchair. She went on until I could stand no more, and for the first time ever I retaliated. I remember exactly what I said.

I said, "Stop it. Stop it, for God's sake. Stop or I'll quiet you for good!" I was amazed at my own outburst.

Then she began to laugh at me and challenged me with "Go on, then – do it. Quiet me for good! You haven't got the guts, you stupid, gutless weakling of a man!'

She laughed again, more of a shrill cackle than a laugh, like a witch, as she smashed her stick across my face. She raised her stick once more, and this time she swept the porcelain figurines off the sideboard with her walking stick – the figurines which I prized so highly – the figurines that my mother had given me on her deathbed! My wife smashed them to smithereens!

Next she said, "Come on, you useless old bugger – kill me. Kill me . . . if you dare!"

I flipped in that second. I've never felt such anger in my life before. It was at this point that some manic power seemed to overwhelm me and a red glaze appeared before my eyes. I went towards Esther to stop her taunts, to shut down the flow of abuse which continued to rush from her lips like a foaming torrent. I put my hands round her neck and I squeezed and squeezed, harder than I had ever squeezed anything in my life before. I cannot say for how long I held on, but when my hands moved away from her neck my fingers were frozen in a cramped, claw-like position. They hurt. I had difficulty in straightening them. There was a thud as Esther's body lolled forward and fell in a heap from the wheelchair on to the floor, trapping my left foot. I extricated my foot with some difficulty. I took a few steps backwards and stared in horrified disbelief at what I had done! I believe I stood there for some time. And then I turned quickly, went out of the room, out of the house and walked and walked – where, I can't remember. At first I thought of going straight to the police. That might have been the best thing to do, but I quickly dismissed the idea, fearful of what might be the outcome!

Some little time later I found myself going up the drive to my house. I opened the door and went into the room where Esther was, to verify that I had indeed killed her, for I could scarcely believe myself capable of such a thing. As I opened the lounge door a ray of moonlight shone full on the dead face of my wife, showing the staring eyes which were still open but glazed and unnatural. She seemed to be watching me as I entered. I went towards her to lift her back into the wheelchair. As I did so, her torso fell forward with a sudden jerk and a last gasp of air came from her lips, accompanied by a low, throaty sound as the remaining air was forced up from her lungs with the pressure of falling forward. At this I sprang back in terror, believing for a moment she was still alive, and I fled to the kitchen and leaned against the sink for support as I felt my strength draining from me. After a few minutes I regained my composure somewhat and forced myself back into the lounge to assure myself that Esther was dead for certain. I touched her cold hand, trying to straighten her fingers where she had clawed at me as I'd strangled her, but I could not move them. Rigor mortis had set in, and I needed no further proof of death.

And now, my dearest Martha, I am about to ask you what I have no right whatsoever to ask, but you are my only hope. I have no one else to turn to. I don't deserve help, I know, but I am like a drowning man clutching at straws. You will see I have put my house key in with this letter – I thought that if you can find it in your heart to help me would you go to my house as if visiting Esther in my absence, so things appear 'normal'? Near neighbours will be aware I am not at home and will be wondering how Esther is managing. I hope to be home in a day or so when I've settled my dead brother's affairs here.

Think carefully, Martha, on what you decide to do, for I wish no harm to come to you in connection with what I have done.

With much love and deepest regrets,

Clive.

So it was that in this impossible situation Clive had decided to appeal to me for help. When I began to read Clive's letter I never expected anything like this! Who would? What an account Clive gave in that letter to me – so detailed too and so shocking! So that's what it was all about the day I saw Clive go off with the police. The second policeman waiting at Clive's door was evidently waiting for nothing more serious than a police car to pick him up to investigate another matter in the opposite direction from where Clive was heading.

I had to reread Clive's letter umpteen times as I found it extremely difficult to digest what it contained, but gradually I began to believe it. And now I determined to put into operation what Clive had really asked of me. It concerned his dead wife, of course. I was to go to Clive's house and pretend to be seeing to his wife's needs. He thought it could be a day or so before he'd be able to get home. Suspicions would be aroused if no one was seen to be going to attend to his wife, for most neighbours were aware of her disability. As you have read, Clive enclosed a front-door key with the letter so there'd be no problem getting into the house. I didn't have to help Clive, of course, but somehow I felt a compulsion to do so. I could have opted to go to the police myself and tell them what I knew, and that would be that. But I couldn't. I'd always felt I wanted to help

Clive, and now here was an opportunity indeed, however unsavoury it might be! It was uncanny how Clive had asked for my help. I'm certain he felt some bond between us, as I had done almost from the first time I met him. Whatever it was, there was no denying there was some magnetic attraction between us!

I didn't hesitate now. Clive really needed someone – and that someone was me! I thought what to do and decided to go over to Clive's house after lunch.

I made a nice beef casserole and filled one of my smaller dishes with the stew. After all, my entire mission must look authentic. I walked over the road just after one, carrying the casserole. I walked slowly – I wanted to be seen by whoever was about. I saw Mrs Jackson was back from wherever it was she'd been. I could feel her eyes on me from behind her net curtains as I turned the key in Clive's door and went in. She'd wonder how I came to be doing this, I knew. I saw Mrs Jackson's curtains move again, but I gave no indication I'd seen her there. I shut the door quickly. I recognised the layout of the house as all the houses in our road were built to the same plan.

My heart began to race as I approached the lounge door. It was only open a couple of inches and the curtains were partly drawn. I pushed the door open slowly. The back of the wheelchair was what I saw first. I went past it and there she was! My God! Clive's wife was wedged almost sideways in her chair, as Clive had left her. She was wearing a beautiful blue silk blouse with the name 'Esther' embroidered on the breast pocket. So that was her name. Funny how Clive had never called her Esther to me – just 'my wife' – but then in his letter he had sometimes referred to her as 'my wife' and sometimes as Esther. 'Another biblical name,' I thought.

Her face had a marble look and she seemed almost statue-like. She wasn't at all like I'd imagined her. She was quite beautiful, even in death! Her hair, which was a rich auburn, had started to go grey at the sides.

What was Clive going to do with her? She couldn't stay there much longer. I put the dish of stew on a small table near the kitchen door, and the dish cover slipped letting out an appetising smell of beef stew. But Esther wouldn't need that or any other food again. And it was then that the idea came to me: the kitchen chest freezer – a very large one. She'd be all right in there, preserved, sort of, until Clive decides what to do with her. I went into the kitchen and opened up the freezer top. It was heavy and creaked uneasily and stayed up at an angle of about seventy degrees. It wouldn't go back any further. I looked in. It was just under half full of meat joints, sausages, chops, frozen vegetables, two large tubs of ice cream and a few other bits. I took the stuff out, piece by piece, and piled it up by the side of the freezer. It took some time, but at last it was done. My hands were so numbed by this time I could hardly feel them. I went back into the lounge.

I'd never done anything like this before, but I dragged Esther's body out of her wheelchair, across the room and into the kitchen. She wasn't so much heavy as awkward. The hardest thing was getting her into the freezer. After several attempts I managed it. She was in. One of her legs stuck out awkwardly, making the fitting-in difficult. I tried to push her leg in next to the other one, but I only succeeded in part, although I pressed with all my strength. I heard a cracking sound and could push the leg no further. She was completely stiff. I began to pile the frozen food back in on top of her until she was just about covered. When I'd finished, the freezer looked quite full as the level of the food had risen so much. Then I put the lid down and forced it shut. She'd keep in there all right.

I didn't panic in the midst of all this. And I had taken the precaution of wearing gloves to avoid leaving fingerprints. Well, Clive had asked for my help and I had given it. How could I have refused? His affect on me was little short of hypnotic. I felt he'd only to suggest something and I'd be drawn to comply. I'd never felt that way about Jim!

That reminds me: I'd better be getting back to him. He'll wonder where I am. He knows my movements and that I only go out on certain days, at certain times. I'm as regular as clockwork, he says. Well, I am as a rule, but it's not every day you're called on to do what I've just done, is it? They say you can do anything if you have to – well, I just did. It wasn't as bad as I thought it was going to be. In fact, I got a bit of a thrill from it all! It was the first thing that had afforded me any excitement for a long time. Well, there was my first encounter with Clive, of course – and ever since – but that was different. He's alive, but his wife – well, she won't trouble anyone again. Funny to think she's said her last word, had her last meal, her last thought . . . And I wonder what that was. I bet she never thought Clive would finish her off; no not Clive, not quiet, inoffensive, forbearing, stupid Clive. It must have been the biggest shock of her life when Clive roused himself and turned on her. They say even a worm will turn. Well, Clive turned all right – with finality, as you might say!

I think that was what attracted me to Clive in the first place, that from his quiet forbearance he could break out if sufficiently provoked. And yet it was me he had asked for help. He must trust me, that's for sure. Or maybe he's a fatalist – believes what will be will be. He must be aware I could shop him right now if I so chose, or protect him. I think he knew which I would choose to do.

I decided I wouldn't walk out of Clive's house with the casserole dish in my hands – better make it look as if I'd really left it for Clive's wife to eat. I'll go back later to collect it – a perfectly natural thing to do, except circumstances are anything but natural!

Chapter 11

I left Clive's house, quietly locking the door behind me.

"All right, all right, I'm coming. No need to knock the floor through with your walking stick, Jim!"

I pretended I'd been in downstairs all the time, so as Jim wouldn't ask any questions.

When I went up to Jim he was crying. I had only seen him do that once before. It was when the cat died. Somebody had put poison down near our house – a kind of weedkiller, I think, and our cat, Captain, had eaten some of it. I was very upset too, of course, but Jim took it very badly.

I asked Jim, "What's wrong?"

"Gone," he said. "Gone!"

I found out after some minutes that Jim meant his 'friend' had gone – the imaginary one he believes sits in the chair opposite to him in his room.

"He's left – gone for good," Jim whined. He was very distressed.

"What is his name, Jim, this friend of yours?" I asked.

"Clive," he said, "just Clive."

That gave me a bit of a start. I don't ever remember telling Jim the neighbour across the road is called Clive. All I said was that I'd seen the man across the road getting into a police car, and Jim said (as I think I mentioned earlier) that it was none of our business, or words to that effect.

Look at him – there he goes again, another black look coming on and he's slavering again. He seems very troubled in his mind. He's like a little child, sobbing fitfully to himself. It's pitiful to see and hear him like this. Let's hope there's some improvement soon, though I don't have much faith that there will be.

**

I call it a spring clean though it's autumn actually! I've given Jim's room a really good clean-out. I was tidying his things when I came across photos of when we got engaged. I found the wedding list of guests too. I showed them to Jim and he asked whose wedding was it going to be? Shame really! Still, they did tell me that he was most unlikely to recall much of the past and his general mental condition was liable to deteriorate further. As you may deduce, this information has been given to me by my partners in crime –the doctors, Smith and Jones. They had particular medical names for Jim's condition which escape me at the moment. Makes no difference what you call it, Jim's still as mad as a hatter and there's no getting away from it.

I've sorted Jim's clothes out too. Some I've discarded. He's got two beautiful new suits, new shirts, shoes, etc., which he has never worn. He'll never wear them now – never goes out anywhere, does he? Then there's his money. Jim never believed in banks even when he was in his right mind. He keeps his money in a portable safe and only Jim knows the combination – that's if he hasn't forgotten it, of course! I do remember Jim telling me when we were engaged something about him having deposited a large sum of money – 'in a safe place', he said, for he had this premonition that one day something terrible would happen to him, or me, or both of us, and he'd need money then. I dismissed what he said as one of his delusions, which he appears to suffer from on occasions! Jim always gave me the impression he wasn't short of a bob or two.

Also I received a considerable amount of money from his three insurance policies when he 'died'. It was thanks to my doctor friends that I got away with the insurance monies being paid out. I wrote them a fairly hefty cheque each for that assistance too.

I've never ceased to be amazed how well the arrangements have gone all these years between me and the doctors. I've got implicit faith in both of them. The one who signed Jim's death certificate was Dr Smith, and you can't have a better name than that to support your anonymity! He'd be struck off the doctors' register if it was found out what we did, and the same goes for Dr Jones. I'd be in desperate straits also for fraudulent practices, etc. Still, so far so good!

**

I don't know what to do. I was just going to bed when I looked out of the window and I saw there was a light on in Clive's house. I say a light, but it was more like occasional flashes from a torch or suchlike. I don't think Clive has returned home yet. He's been gone over three days now. He would surely have contacted me if he is indeed at home. Esther could hardly have shown a light, could she? I wonder if I should go and investigate. I have been over there twice since putting Esther in the freezer, just to keep up the pretence of helping her. It's gone midnight now. I can't sleep and that's for sure. I'll make a cup of tea. The Brits' cure for every worry, they say!

Ah! That's better. The tea does help. Quarter to one now. Good heavens! The light in Clive's house – it's gone, and yet I'm certain Clive isn't at home. Who has turned a light on in his house, then? It's two days now since I put Esther in the freezer. She'll be solid all right, but it will preserve her. I don't like to think about that too much. No, I won't go over there at this late hour. I'll wait till tomorrow. I'll try to get some sleep.

Chapter 12

Oh, my head! It feels so heavy. Anybody would think I'd been on the bottle all night. I've just taken Jim a cup of tea. He says he doesn't want any breakfast, again! He was sitting muttering to himself. I'll take the paper to him when I've seen it myself. I can't tell if he makes much of it, but he seems to like to see it. Ah, it's just arrived. I wish that paper boy wouldn't screw the paper up when he posts it through the letter box. They just don't care these days.

It was the right-hand side of the front page that caught my eye. It was in the 'Stop Press'. It read, 'Body of Disabled Woman Found in Freezer after House Break-in'. My God! That's Esther!

I waited till five o'clock, and later that evening I bought the *Evening Gazette*. And there it was again: 'Body in Freezer'. But in much more detail, of course. A break-in at Clive's and a dead body – well, there's food for thought!

It seems an anonymous phone call alerted police to suspicious goings-on at the property across from me – Clive's property. Anyone who has seen or heard anything suspicious in that area, however trivial, is to contact the police immediately.

I did that very thing.

"Yes, officer that's right. When I went over to see her she was fine. I had gone to take her some lunch over. I've been taking meals to the house while her husband's been away. I expect you know that her husband was informed of his brother's tragic death in an accident and he has gone to identify the body and so on. So very sad! I did offer to stay the night with his wife, her being so incapacitated, but she insisted I went home. She said she could manage. So I left her and locked the door behind me. Her husband left me a key. He thought he might be away a day or so to settle his brother's business affairs, and, as you must know, he isn't back yet."

I also told the police about the flashing light I had seen the previous night at Clive's. I said I thought maybe Clive had come home very late, but of course we believed he was still away. The police asked me if I had anything further to tell them.

At this point I pretended to break down – understandable in the circumstances – and I said, between sobs, "This awful, awful crime must have happened in the night. Poor, poor Esther! I should never have left her! God forgive me – why didn't I stay with her? If I had, this dreadful crime would never have happened! It must have been intruders who broke in and did this dreadful deed! Oh, my God, I feel so guilty! If only, if only . . ." followed by more deep sobs.

The police were very sympathetic. "There there, madam. Don't distress yourself. It does look at the moment as if the break-in resulted in your poor neighbour meeting her end, but we have to prove it. Thank you for your help. You can be certain justice will be done."

And he hung up.

It was surely something of a bonus that there had been a break-in at Clive's house and a dead body was found there, for it did look to all intents and purposes as if the intruders into Clive's property were responsible for Esther's death. I expect the intruders went in there to see what they could steal. I did hear later that a few valuables were taken, but they may have been disturbed before they could find more. Or maybe they looked in the freezer for some reason and made a hasty exit! And Clive wasn't even home when the break-in occurred!

I've been mulling over what Clive did. It was indeed a terrible thing to do, but I believe he is more to be pitied than blamed. 'A man more sinned against than sinning' came to mind just then. Memories of *King Lear* many moons ago. Jim had a small part in that Shakespeare play, I recall. Looking at the state Jim is in now, it's hard to realise the person he used to be! If he was in his right mind, I wonder what he'd make of what I did for Clive over the road.

There is one good thing about the police investigation, and it is this: there will be none of my fingerprints on Esther or the freezer as I took the precaution of wearing gloves, didn't I? My prints will only be on the front door and maybe the table by the wheelchair, which would be quite normal for anyone delivering a meal to Esther. I didn't put the gloves on until I came to move Esther to the freezer. Clive would be in the clear too, for Clive had strangled Esther with his hands on the scarf she wore round her neck. She always wore it because of her arthritis – it seemed to afford her some relief. So Clive's prints would not be visible on her neck, and later he told me he took the precaution of removing the scarf and taking it out with him. Little did they know, but the intruders had provided a near perfect alibi! The police suspected them of murder and Clive wasn't even there, was he?

Chapter 13

"Isn't it absolutely awful? Right next door to me as well. You're just not safe in your own home these days. If only I'd been at home myself I might have been able to do something. I'm sure I'd have known if something funny was going on in the night, but I was staying at my sister's, you see. I went just after I saw you going in Clive's with a dish or something. Giving her a dinner, were you? It was me who phoned the police, you know, though evidently someone phoned the police before me even! I saw all about the dreadful business in the paper. I mean, living next door I thought it was my duty to contact the police. Not that I could tell them much – I wasn't there, was I? Oh, my God, when I think of it! I told the police about all the rows and screaming that went on at Clive's house. I heard from the police that the back door was forced. Must have been how the beggars got in.

"I can't quite take it all in. Fancy a murder and right next door to me! I feel quite faint, dear. I suppose you must have been the last one to see Esther alive! Clive's just come home, you know. He must be in a terrible state of shock! First his brother, then his wife! You don't think that Clive could possibly have . . . No, of course he couldn't. He wasn't even there, was he? Not that anyone would blame him really with what he had to put up with. You never can tell, can you, dear? Must fly. See you later". And she was gone, with her usual sudden exit. Mrs Jackson, as you must have guessed!

Clive's house must be cursed. One died in it suddenly – poor old Mr Olsen – then his wife went out shopping and was never seen again right up to this day! And now this! They say things go in threes.

That reminds me: I've given Jim his breakfast and I've put his clean clothes out, but he hasn't had his tablets yet. I can't do with him missing his tablets. They help to keep him calm, you know. He's been getting more and more agitated lately – the least thing sends him off. I might need to double Jim's dosage – that should do the trick – but I'll see how he goes on for a bit longer. And that's one more thing I have to thank Dr Smith and Dr Jones for: Jim's medication. They send me Jim's tablets at regular intervals. I don't think I could manage Jim without them.

Jim's been giving me funny looks for the past day or two when I go into his room. It's like he has an idea I've been up to something. The trouble is there's just no way of knowing just how much he does understand nowadays. He might be taking in more than I think. He asked me for writing paper and an envelope the other day, and a stamp. I didn't ask him what he wanted it for. I don't expect him to do anything with it. He'll have forgotten all about it by tomorrow, I suppose. It'll just be one of his 'fancies'. I just try to humour him and we manage, more or less. I gave him what he asked for, but so far I haven't seen any evidence of a letter.

I took Jim a big dish of his favourite ice cream again today, but, just like yesterday, he pushed it away from him and began to shake violently. Also he's done a lot more mumbling incoherently lately – mumbo-jumbo again. So it's very hard now for us to have a conversation. I've almost given up trying. I just try to please him as best I can, but it's difficult.

I couldn't tell whether Jim liked his birthday or not this year. He waved the budgerigar away, so I've got the bird downstairs. I can't think Jim is now fifty-six! He looks more like seventy-six, so gaunt and wild-looking. He slavers a lot more often now too – can't seem to control it. He didn't even touch the birthday cake I made him. His appetite has been poor for some time now. He actually threw a plate at me today when I took the ice cream in! I shan't take him any more. Fortunately I swerved to avoid it, so it missed me, smashing against the wall.

Chapter 14

I see Clive's back. He'll know I received his letter and he'll have been informed of the break-in at his house and about the intruders who are suspects for the murder of his wife. After a thorough search of the house, Esther's body was indeed found in the freezer. She's been removed to a police mortuary for further examination. Clive must be desperate to talk to me. I'll go across as soon as I can.

I plucked up courage and went over to Clive's this evening. He opened the door before I knocked. He must have seen me coming.

We were both equally aware that Mrs Jackson was watching as usual, so I said, in a voice I knew she'd hear, "Just came to see if I could do anything."

"Come in," Clive said.

I slipped inside and closed the door quietly.

"You did it – you helped me, Martha! Oh, Martha, you dear, sweet person," he said.

Without any previous intention of doing so, I found myself holding on to Clive very tightly and he to me. Neither of us spoke for some time – we just held one another. It was more of a need in each of us to draw courage and strength from one another at this highly charged, emotional moment – an effort, jointly, to justify and maybe find forgiveness for what had taken place in this house so recently.

I'm not sure how long we stayed locked together, and in a way time seemed irrelevant, but slowly we relaxed our hold on each other and walked separately into the lounge – the room where 'it' had all taken place.

It looked brighter. The wheelchair had gone. The curtains were drawn back a little, letting in shafts of bright moonlight. For no particular reason we sat in the half-light.

I spoke first: "After I got your letter, Clive, I made up my mind to help you if I could, shattered as I naturally was at what had happened here. I thought it best to make things appear as normal as possible. So although I knew Esther was – Esther was – dead" – I swallowed hard here and I know my voice faltered – "I came over as if bringing her something to eat. I know Mrs Jackson saw me carrying the casserole dish in here. There was so much to read in your letter, Clive. It was like a horror story. Oh, Clive, it was awful coming in here. I couldn't believe what had happened. When I read what you wrote, I kept thinking, 'You, of all people!' but I can understand now that it's because you're you that it happened. You were driven to it. I know you never *meant* to kill Esther – it was never deliberate."

There were a few seconds of silence, then Clive spoke: "Oh, Martha, you'll never know how very much I've wanted, these last few days, someone to say what you have just said. Believe me, I never intended to kill her. Even in my worst days with Esther, I never – as God is my Judge, I never intended to harm her. But I did . . . It happened! Something in my mind just snapped. I lost control. It's done and nothing can undo this dreadful deed!"

Clive paced jerkily up and down by the window as he spoke, like someone in a torment of mind, as if an inner demon was tearing at his soul. Then, in contrast, he went quiet for several minutes.

After what seemed an age I broke the silence with "I thought it best to put Esther in the chest freezer, Clive. I didn't know when you'd be back."

"You did well there," he said. "That was very clever of you, and brave! It's helped in other ways too: the low temperature may have made her death and the bruising on her neck appear a little more recent, and that may be another reason the police suspect it was the intruders who strangled her. It's ironic how events have turned out. Yes, the break-in here could have done us a big favour! You'll never know how much I value your help, Martha. You've been my salvation in all of this. I feel more certain than ever that fate has brought us together. It wasn't me who chose to live opposite you; I truly believe I was guided here, and that it was previously ordained that it should be so. Tell me, Martha: don't you feel the same? Tell me that you do. I've known for weeks and weeks that there's some strange, inexplicable bond drawing us together. It's as if it's all beyond our control and maybe not of our choosing. Tell me, Martha, that you feel at least a little of this."

I said nothing at first, then I said, "Yes, Clive, you're right – there is something . . . something . . . a feeling, a power I've never felt before with anyone else and I can't explain it. It scares me to think what may come of it all, yet it's wonderful too."

"Don't be afraid, Martha. I'll always be near when you need someone. Let that suffice for the present," Clive said.

And I knew, as he spoke, that we must both bide our time, awaiting whatever might be ahead of us.

"We must be very careful, Clive. Things are a long way off being settled. The police don't give up easily. They won't be satisfied till they've sifted every bit of evidence regarding Esther's death. They've yet to find the intruders, and if they do I wonder what they'll have to say."

"What have we to fear, Martha? The intruders surely are the only suspects as far as the police are concerned. No, Martha, for the first time in a long, long time I feel as if a great burden has been lifted from me," Clive said. With this he gave a tremendous sigh as if by that he expelled all worries from his system.

"I only wish I could feel as positive about everything as you do, Clive, but we must just bide our time, I suppose. But in all this trouble, Clive, you haven't told me how you got on regarding your brother's fatal accident. I'm so sorry he was killed. You never mentioned this brother to me before."

"No, Martha, I didn't. This was my older brother, Brian. We've had very little contact with one another for years. I'm afraid some might say Brian is the black sheep of the family, always in trouble from his teenage years and throughout his life. He spent several years in prison, I'm afraid, for robberies and suchlike – including GBH, I'm sad to say. When he came out he was a loner and none of our family knew his whereabouts. It seems he stole the car which killed him, but the police found some papers on him naming me as next of kin should anything happen to him. So that's how the police came to contact me. My family tried so many times in the past to help Brian, but he spurned them and went his own way."

41

"That's very sad, Clive – very sad indeed," I said.

"It is, Martha. I'll have to sort out Brian's funeral too as well as Esther's, though I don't know when the police will release her body for burial. What a dark passage we're going through just now! What else can go wrong?"

I didn't answer. I went into the kitchen and saw that my casserole dish was intact among all the chaos caused by the intruders. Clive had been warned not to touch anything until the police had completed their investigations, but he'd evidently been given the all-clear just before I arrived. They'd checked for fingerprints everywhere, and they found mine on the casserole dish, on the kitchen table and in a few other places, and dismissed them as quite normal. They'd been particularly interested in the prints they couldn't account for – those belonging to the burglars, presumably.

"I must go now, Clive," I said.

"I know, dearest Martha, you have worries of your own with Jim, besides what I've got you involved in here," Clive said. "That's why I truly appreciate all the more the help you've given me at this horrendous time. I'm not expressing myself very well, am I? My words are so inadequate to say what I really mean, my dearest Martha, for you must surely know that is what you are to me – dear, very dear indeed! I will repay you, Martha, in time, in whatever ways I can. I know what I hope for the future, but now is not the time or place to think on these things."

I think I knew what Clive meant by these last few words.

"I really must go now, Clive, but please, please be careful!" I squeezed his hand gently in reassurance and left.

I went home, taking the casserole dish with me. Mrs Jackson must have been timing my stay in Clive's house. She was still peeping from behind her curtains. So what? I'd merely been to collect my dish, hadn't I? It would only be natural to stay a while and discuss the recent happenings. She'd have been more suspicious probably if I'd gone straight in and out again.

Chapter 15

There was a strong smell of paint, or something similar, as I entered the house. It hit me forcibly as I walked through the hall. It was coming from upstairs. I put my dish down and hurried up the stairs. I felt panicky for some reason. I went into Jim's room – he wasn't there. "Jim, Jim, where are you? Jim, answer me!" I must have sounded almost hysterical.

Jim seldom left his room unless he was in the spare room doing his woodwork. He kept that door locked more often than not – so I couldn't know what he got up to, I suppose. It was then I heard something coming from the spare room. The door was slightly open. I pushed it further. Yes, there he was, busy dismantling bits of furniture I'd got him from an auction sometime ago. Jim didn't say anything to me – just gave me a weird kind of half-smile. Then I saw it: a half-made coffin!

Why a second coffin? I wondered. He seemed obsessed with making coffins. So that's what all the banging and sawing and stink of glue-making had been about over the past few weeks.

Jim looked as if he expected me to comment on his work, so I said, "Very nice, Jim. You're a clever workman, but what is it for? You've made one coffin already."

He didn't answer, merely smiled inanely and made a kind of hissing sound followed by a massive slavering which concertinaed from the left side of his mouth, finally dropping in a frothy blob as it gathered weight. Then he pushed me out of the spare room, locking the door behind him, and slithered unsteadily into his own room. I left him and went downstairs.

Mrs Jackson's been over here every afternoon for the past week telling me of the comings and goings of the police to and from Clive's house. She didn't need to bother – I've seen it all for myself. Well, I'm a very interested party, aren't I? I had a visitor myself yesterday. It was a police inspector – not anybody I saw when I was at the police station the other day. He just wanted to verify that what I said in my statement at the station was correct, and had I anything else to add? No, I hadn't. It was exactly as I'd told it originally. Better stick to what I'd said in the first place!

He thanked me, then he left. I don't know why exactly, but I didn't feel at all comfortable after the visit. It seems strange so long after the 'event' getting bad nerves. I reckoned my confidence should have grown, but just the opposite appears to be the case. I had a brandy to steady myself – a thing I've never done before. The effect was that I became more unsteady, but for a different reason! I went to bed, forgetting to give Jim his medication.

There was a bit in the paper today about Clive's wife. It said the inquest is to be on Thursday – oh, God, that's tomorrow! It also said that so far no sign has been found of those responsible for breaking into Clive's house. The police are continuing with their enquiries and still suspect the intruders of killing Clive's wife. As Clive explained to the police that not much has been stolen from the house, it is thought the burglars panicked and maybe strangled Esther when she challenged them.

I decided to go and see how Clive was coping. I hadn't seen him come out of the house since I was over there last, a few days ago. I had to go out anyway. Jim gave me to understand he wanted more wood for his 'work'. I knew the auction rooms would be open that afternoon, so I might pick up something useful for him. Funny thing was Jim was speaking almost coherently today when he asked me to get him the wood – oak, I should say. He insisted it must be oak. I once tried to fool him with some oak-faced drawers, but it didn't work. He knows the difference all right!

Clive's door was slightly open as I knocked gently and walked in. It was the first time I'd gone in the back way.

"Martha! Oh, Martha, I'd begun to think you'd abandoned me" he said.

He reached out and drew me towards him in a close embrace. It seemed the most natural thing in the world to both of us at that moment. The closeness gave way to a feeling of great comfort and peace between us – a feeling in great contrast to the grim events which brought us so close together in the first place.

"Oh, Clive, how could you think I'd abandon you? How could I put aside, even for one minute, what we've shared in here of late? It's just that in view of everything I thought it wiser to stay away for a little while. As I've said before, we have to be extremely careful for things are a long way from settled yet."

Clive made no comment on what I said, but in answer he took both my hands in his and raised them to his lips.

It was almost a reverence.

"Forgive me, dear, dear Martha. You bring such light into the darkness of my life. You ask nothing for yourself, and yet you have helped me so much. I realise we have known each other so short a time, and yet such a bond has grown between us which, for me, gathers strength as each day goes by. I would never forgive myself if out of all that's happened any harm should come to you. You must not mind that I speak so. There is more – so much more – than a deep friendship between us."

And he released my hands from his firm grasp.

"Clive, I know there is this strong bond between us. I have felt it for some time, although we've spoken little of it. Funny how you don't need words for such things – you just know. But don't worry over me, Clive – you've had more than your share of worry and heartache. I helped you because I wanted to. I didn't have to. No one forced me. It was entirely my decision. It's true I've been drawn towards you, as you to me, ever since the first day I saw you, I think – that day at the bus stop, remember? I never thought for one moment I'd ever feel towards anyone the way I feel about you – and me with poor Jim to look after! – but that's how things are."

I remained silent for a moment or so. Clive sighed long and loud. We went into the lounge. Clive had changed the furniture around.

"You noticed?" he said. "I couldn't bear to look at it all as it was when she – when Esther . . . Oh, God, Martha!"

And he sobbed uncontrollably, like a child, as he fell to his knees and laid his cheek on my lap, wetting my dress with his tears.

"Sob away, Clive, if it helps you. You mustn't blame yourself so much for what happened here. Yes, it was very wrong, but many others would have acted the same in your position. When you could stand the constant abuse no longer, Clive, you snapped. I know you never planned to kill Esther."

I don't think what I said helped Clive's remorse. With a tremendous effort, Clive composed himself somewhat and kept apologising for his outburst. Then he sat very quietly. I tried to comfort him as best I could, stroking the tears from his wet cheeks. It was like consoling a child who has undergone a terrifying experience. I felt almost motherly towards him, which was strange, of course, as I've never had a child of my own. But they say all that kind of thing is born in us anyway. It was over five minutes before either of us broke the silence.

Then Clive said, "It's the inquest, you see. It's tomorrow. I'm dreading it. I don't suppose . . . No, you couldn't, could you?"

"Come with you, Clive? I don't think that would be wise," I told him.

"No, of course not. You're right, Martha. I'm a coward, I suppose, and that's the truth of it. Pray for me, Martha – especially tomorrow!"

"I will," I said, and I meant it.

I'd never put Clive down as a particularly religious person, but don't we all call on God for help when we're in desperate situations? They say God forgives anything if we are truly repentant. We'll just have to wait and see in this case.

The inquest hearing was for three o'clock evidently. I saw Clive leave his house just after two the next day. He looked to have aged ten years in the past few weeks. I felt a great urge to be with him at the inquest, to offer my support, but I knew I mustn't.

Chapter 16

I couldn't settle to anything that day. I went to the auction rooms and managed to buy some pieces of oak. It was actually a broken oak chest. I think Jim will be pleased with that. They said they'd deliver it later in the day. I spent more than I intended to on the chest, but I bought it all the same. It would keep Jim occupied, I knew. There was very little else that pleased him nowadays.

The chest was indeed delivered late that evening. They even carried it to the top of the stairs for me. Jim looked it over. You could never tell exactly what he thought about things. He merely pointed to his mother's deed box, which told me he wanted to pay for the chest. I didn't argue with that. Jim took a small key from his pocket as I handed him the deed box. He opened it and counted out the money I'd told him the chest had cost. It didn't look like there was much money left in Jim's box. I took the money from him. I'd managed to bring quite a few of Jim's belongings from the place where he used to live before they put him in that psychiatric ward years ago, and Jim's mother's deed box was one of them.

I'd just sent my quarterly 'charge' to my doctor friends, so my current account was down a bit more than I would have liked. I'd better be transferring some money from one of my other accounts as I've never yet been overdrawn and I've no intention of starting now! My legacy money was mostly invested in stocks and shares, which are doing very nicely, and I am reluctant to cash in any of those at present.

I made myself a pot of tea and sat down at the kitchen table to drink it. I thought over all that had happened in the past few months. It seemed unbelievable, but deep down I knew it was all true enough. If anyone had forecast any of this six months ago, I would have said they were off their heads and no mistake. It was such a strange mixture of joy and guilt that I felt now, both at the same time – joy in my new-found affection for Clive and guilt in knowing I was instrumental in helping him cover up his wife's murder! You can't just blot out something like that – a death. It's so final! You've never to be given a second chance – neither the victim nor the killer. And that's what gets to you. If only, if only! But it will never be any different, and Clive and I are both keenly aware of this.

"You'll just have to make the best of a bad job" my mother used to tell us.

Well, that might help in some matters, but it would hardly help in our case. And yet I would never have got to know Clive so intimately if it hadn't been for the way his wife treated him. No, that's not so – I'd still feel the same about him, I know, if she was still alive. There is just something about Clive that I can't ignore. This is the only time I've felt truly happy with someone, but it's fouled up by all these complications. I never had such feelings for poor Jim, even when he was in his right mind. It was more of a fondness and a friendship. My difficulties may be one of God's little jokes, testing me after my 'wickedness'. My mother called all difficulties 'good for your soul, dear', but I don't think I believe that any more.

I felt myself falling into a doze.

After a few minutes' quiet I jerked violently, the cause being a loud ratatat on the back door. It gave me quite a turn. When I opened the back door there was a lady I'd never seen before asking me if I'd seen a black-and-white cat in the area. She'd evidently lost it. I said I was sorry but I couldn't help her, and she went on her way.

It was at this moment that I turned my thoughts to Jim. I've been getting more concerned about him of late. I realised he hadn't eaten what I would call a decent meal for some time now – not since I'd—

"Stop it!" I told myself.

How could there possibly be any connection?

***

"Here you are, Jim. You'll enjoy this. I made it especially for you – egg custard. The pastry is just as you like it, nicely browned."

Jim gave me that weird, almost sinister, half-smile again, but said nothing. I placed the tray beside him on the little table as usual. Hm! That egg custard smelled really good with the nutmeg sprinkled on top. I got wafts of it in waves. And then there was the teapot, milk jug and sugar basin, all in hammered pewter, not forgetting the willow-pattern cup, saucer and plate. They all belonged to Jim's mother, and he inherited them from her along with several other items. Not that Jim remembers they were his mother's. She has been dead for years, his father likewise. But for some reason Jim will never use any other than these particular bits of crockery, so he must have made some small connection with them and their origin somewhere along the line. They've been on his tray day in and day out now for the past ten years. It is a miracle none of them has been broken or even damaged in the slightest. I've had many other breakages in the kitchen, but somehow Jim's tray items always escape harm.

I didn't wait to see if Jim ate his food, and I've given up for the most part spending my evening hour with him. It doesn't seem to do any good – to Jim or to me. As I've said, most of the time Jim is incoherent or else he sits there looking blank. I've had a new feeling of late too when I've been in his room – a feeling of hostility, a feeling almost of hate at times. It is as if Jim has suddenly taken a strong dislike to me. Well, if he has there isn't much I can do about it. I've always done my best for him. No need to have a conscience on that score, I think. But I still don't feel completely at ease about Jim, although I keep telling myself there is nothing more I can do to help him.

This evening I began to wonder what it would be like without him. I'd miss him – well, naturally after all these years. There would be no worry over Clive though, would there? I could . . . We could . . .

It was at this point that I got a sudden twinge of conscience. What had come over me? Whatever was I thinking about? I determined to put such thoughts out of my head – for the present, at least.

I scanned next day's papers for any news there might have been about the inquest on Clive's wife, but I didn't find anything.

'Perhaps tomorrow,' I told myself.

Chapter 17

"Are you there dear?"

It was Mrs Jackson. She'd taken to giving the smallest of taps on the back door and letting herself in lately. I wish she wouldn't do that – she's in before I know it. I'll have to keep that back door locked.

"So they'll let her be laid to rest now, dear. About time too, I should say."

"Who? Who to rest?" I asked.

"Why, Clive's wife, of course! My! I don't believe you've heard a word I've said. Whatever's wrong? You don't look too well, dear – not your usual self." Mrs Jackson prattled on.

"Oh, I'm all right. I've been suffering with bad headaches on and off lately, that's all," I told her.

Mrs Jackson's reply to this was "I'll put the kettle on, shall I? I'll make us both a nice cuppa. I expect it's that Jim of yours who's getting you down, dear. I mean, I did warn you – don't say I didn't, dear. I said to you that one of these days you'll go down with something. Headaches, you say? Bad ones? Well, of course that's how my cousin Mary started – awful, it was! She only lasted three weeks from start to finish. Mind you, we all gave her a good send-off. Beautiful it was. She'd really have enjoyed it if she could have been there. Well, I mean, she was there and yet she wasn't if you know what I mean, dear. Here – have your cuppa and never mind saying you don't take sugar. I've put two in there – give you the energy to cope, dear!"

'God, doesn't she go on!' I thought.

"Did you say Clive's wife's funeral will take place soon?" I asked.

"Yes, dear. That's what I came over to tell you: it's on Thursday next at eleven o' clock, I heard, at the crematorium, I think, though I'm not absolutely certain if it'll be there. They do say she might have to be buried in the cemetery – you know, with her being murdered as she was, by person or persons unknown. So far, that is, eh! Just in case they have to have her up again for further evidence or suchlike," said Mrs Jackson.

"Stop it! Stop it! It's too horrible," I screamed out, crying all the time. "Please go now. Leave me alone!" I shouted.

"Oh, very well. Here's a turn-up for the books. Sorry, I'm sure, dear – didn't mean to upset you. I can't think why you should be in such a state about things. I mean, you hardly knew the poor soul – well, not till nearly the end – did you? Still, I expect it was a shock, you knowing you were the last one to see her alive most probably. Don't take it too hard, dear – we all have to go sometime. That reminds me: I must fly now, I'm expecting the plumber. Bye, dear. Cheer up, now!"

And she was gone.

Chapter 18

Thursday, did she say? Just a week after the inquest. I must go over and see Clive. I wonder how the inquest went? It must have been awful for Clive. The sooner next Thursday's business is over the better – for him and for me! What's done cannot be undone. You'd think I'd done it myself the way I get so agitated about everything.

'Suspicion always haunts the guilty mind!' Oh, God, there goes another! Fancy me recalling that one – Shakespeare's *Henry VI, Part 3* if I recall correctly. My cousin had a main part in that; yes, that's right, and Jim and I had very minor parts in it. Why, that must be twenty years ago now!

My mind's in such a mix-up lately. I begin to imagine myself in trouble with the law concerning my part in helping Clive, and it could well become a reality yet!

My imagination reaches fever pitch at times, and I can hear myself calling out, "I didn't do it, my lord. I swear it wasn't me! Yes, I did put the body in the freezer, but she was already dead, my lord."

I must stop this or I'll drive myself crazy. I could end up like Jim if I let things get the better of me. No, I must never do that – there's Clive to think about too. I must go over and talk to him. He's only ever been over here the once – that time he needed a cold-water bandage for his wife's foot. I half thought he might have come over, but I know he won't. He's still very insular in spite of everything. Still, he's had years of indoctrination in the art by that wife of his. I don't mean her any disrespect by that remark – it would be wicked to bear her any kind of malice now. I truly hope her spirit is at peace. She is at least one step ahead of us all in spite of everything in that respect. No one can deny the fact. But I'm getting morbid. I must stop it at once.

I waited till it got dark before I went to see Clive. I saw Mrs Jackson's lights go out at half past ten, so shortly after this I went quietly across the road. I'd seen Jim was fast asleep. He'd had his sleeping pills, so I knew he wouldn't stir until morning. I went round the back of Clive's house and was just about to tap on the window when I almost screamed out as a hand held on to my shoulder from behind.

"Sh! It's only me, Martha. Sorry if I scared you. I've just been down the garden to make sure the fire's out in the rubbish I've been burning. I was hoping to see you. Let's go indoors."

It was Clive all right who had given me such a fright! I had to sit down on the first available seat when I got into Clive's kitchen.

"You OK, Martha?" he asked, "Sorry to scare you. I didn't think, my dear."

"Yes, I'm fine. I'm afraid I've been letting things get on top of me, what with what's happened here and the inquest and everything. Oh, Clive, I was so worried about you that I haven't been able to think straight. I came here late as I didn't want Mrs Jackson seeing me. You know what she's like. I can't help wondering if she knows more than she lets on about. But you know why I'm really here, don't you, Clive?" I said.

"Yes, Martha, I've a pretty good idea: the inquest."

At this point Clive motioned me into the lounge and we both sat down. He had half a glass of sherry on the go, so he poured one for me.

Taking a deep breath, Clive began: "The inquest was no picnic, I can tell you. They asked me so many questions I got rather confused. I think they put it down to the state of shock I was supposed to be in still, knowing that someone had murdered Esther."

"But, Clive, it's true you were, and still are, in a state of shock after Esther's death. There's no denying that," I told him, "not to mention your brother's death in an accident. Anybody would be traumatised."

"I know, Martha but I'm in shock because it was me who did it – me who strangled Esther. I killed her, Martha. I still can't believe it! Anyway, the coroner did his summing-up and declared Esther's death to be by strangulation by person or persons as yet unknown. He asked the doctors present if they were agreeable to releasing the body for burial and they said they were. So the funeral is to be next Thursday. Next Monday will be my brother's funeral. It's like a nightmare, Martha."

"Is it to be a cremation for Esther, then, Clive?" I asked.

"It seems not. It was stipulated by the coroner and the police that Esther's body must be buried in case fresh evidence comes to light about her death. They have a special part of the cemetery here for such cases, and that's where she'll be laid to rest."

"What do you mean, Clive, 'such cases'?" I asked.

"Anyone who has met their death by unnatural means – I think that's how they put it. Anyone murdered, just as Esther was!" said Clive. "My brother is being buried in the same cemetery, but in another area."

"Look, Clive – let's face facts: we're in this together and we won't make it if we weaken now. Esther's gone and nothing anyone can do will bring her back. She led you a dance all right while she was here; nevertheless I wish her to be at peace. I wouldn't wish her anything else. You never meant to do it – no one could possibly think that. We've both to pull ourselves together and be strong. We've come this far and we mustn't weaken now. What do you say, Clive?"

I could see my words heartened him somewhat.

"You're right, Martha, though it's easier said than done. You talk of facing facts, but all I'm sure of as we sit here together is the good feelings we have for one another – at least that is something strong and beautiful. I hope you feel the same, Martha."

"You know I do, Clive. Sometimes I think I'm dreaming and I'll waken up and find none of this is real."

As I said this, Clive put his arms round me, holding me close as if to reassure me of his feelings.

"It's real all right, Martha – very real for me. I don't need to tell you, I'm sure, that I love you – love you very deeply, Martha. I know we have only known one another for a comparatively short time, but that doesn't make a scrap of difference. I feel you are what I have been searching for all my life. Does that sound silly, Martha?"

"No, Clive, it sounds beautiful," I said.

"You've begun to mean so very much to me, Martha, and I care so deeply for you. I only want what is good for you. I know we have many obstacles in our way at present, but my hope is that one day we'll make it together; and that puts new meaning into my life. No matter how long it takes, Martha, I'll wait and be glad. My most earnest wish is that you feel the same," said Clive.

"Oh, I do, Clive, I do. You must know that by now," I said, and I kissed him.

It was a moment of true oblivion for both of us, and God knows there is much we'd like to forget! Neither of us said anything for a while, and I took a long, slow sip of my sherry.

It was me who spoke first: "It's a funny old affair, isn't it, Clive? I don't suppose many romances have started off in such tragic circumstances, do you?"

"No, I suppose not. Give me your promise, Martha, that, no matter what, we'll be together one day. If your feelings are as strong as mine, then you will never doubt it, my darling."

"They are, Clive. I love you more than anyone I have ever met before. It's strange really that I've had to wait until so late in life to find such happiness! I wish we could just disappear from our surroundings right now and simply be together, away from everyone we know," I said.

"Let's do that. Oh, Martha, what a wonderful idea!" said Clive.

"Just a wild dream, Clive – that's all it is. No, you know as well as I do we must be sensible, especially in view of all that has happened. And there's my Jim, of course – I don't know what would become of him, I'm sure. No, Clive, we'll have a long, long wait, but true love doesn't fade away. Waiting can only make it stronger," I told him. "Let's get the funerals over – that will be very hard for you, Clive. Oh, by the way, on a lighter note perhaps, Mrs Jackson's been going round the neighbours collecting for flowers, so don't be surprised!"

All of a sudden there was a knock at the door.

"Oh, my God, Clive, who can that be at this hour of the night? It's almost midnight," I said in a panic.

"Stay there – I'll go and see."

And Clive went to the front door.

Chapter 19

"Oh, God! Oh, Clive, thank God you're still up! Oh, I'm so terrified. Come quickly! I saw you'd got your light on. I swear someone's got into my house. I heard the handle turn on my bedroom door and I heard heavy breathing. I'm certain I wasn't imagining it. Oh, my God, I could have been done in!"

"Let's have a look," Clive said.

As he walked with Mrs Jackson, I heard Clive ask if she had rung the police. I couldn't hear any more after that. I waited a minute or so. I looked over the road at my house and then I saw it: a light on at the side of the house, upstairs, shining out of the spare room. I knew I'd never have left a light on in there. It couldn't be – no, it couldn't be Jim. He'd had his sleeping pills! I had to get back over there right away.

I hastened out of Clive's house and over to mine. At the same moment Mrs Jackson came out of her front door with Clive. She surely must have seen the back of me disappearing down the path to the back of my house, though she'd only have seen me as a dark moving shape, I know. She couldn't know who it was. At least, I hope she couldn't!

Then I heard her scream: "Look! Look over there! He's over there now. I told you there was someone – I didn't imagine it!"

"There's no one there, now calm yourself – I assure you there's no one in your house. Go in, take a couple of tablets and go to bed," Clive told her.

"Maybe there's nobody in there now, but there was, I tell you. There was, and now whoever it was has gone in the direction of Martha's house!"

With that she went indoors, locking her front door noisily and slamming home the several bolts that also secured her property.

***

When Clive went indoors he found Martha gone. He looked out of his lounge window just in time to see a light going out in an upstairs room in Martha's house.

'Oh well,' he thought, 'I expect Martha got a bit panicky with Mrs Jackson's visit here. At least I have something precious to live for now. Martha loves me almost as much as I love her, I believe, and there's the future ahead; but it could be a very, very long wait indeed!'

Clive went to bed thinking sweet thoughts of his beloved Martha.

***

Oh no, he can't have – but he has. Jim's been up after I went over to Clive's, but how could he after taking his sleeping tablets? He did take them – or did he? Well, I left them beside him on the bedside cabinet. Maybe he didn't take them, after all. He certainly appeared fast asleep when I checked and the tablets had gone. I wonder what he's been up to? I know I didn't put a light on in the spare room. Jim keeps it locked most of the time anyway, and I haven't got a spare key. I went to the spare room and – surprise, surprise! – the door was ajar. Well, just look – would you believe it? He's dragged that old chest of drawers in here and dismantled it almost. Now, I wonder what on earth inspired him to start on that so late at night. He's been getting too devious for my liking of late. I'll have to watch him more closely in future. I'll just see if he's really asleep now.

I looked in on Jim, and there he was fast asleep this time for certain. Maybe he'd hidden his pills away somewhere and only just took them a short while ago.

I expect Clive wondered about my sudden departure. It's a pity he's not on the phone. We could be a comfort to one another that way. When I asked him about it, he said his wife didn't hold with having phones. "An intrusion into your privacy," she'd told Clive.

He always obeyed her to the letter. Maybe if he'd stood up to her in the earlier years of their marriage she wouldn't have become so domineering

57

towards him. Still, I wouldn't have wanted that, would I? We might never have had the chance to meet and fall in love as we have done.

I went to bed thinking about Clive and me. It is a strange affair, I must admit. Some people wouldn't think much of it, I know. Most people's idea of a romance is about going out, spending money, being thoroughly idolised and pursuing all the pleasures available to us here on earth. Well, it was hardly like that for Clive and me, which I think makes our love all the more valuable. Just knowing we care deeply for one another is sufficient, each of us wishing for the well-being, peace and happiness of the other.

We don't need material things to back it up. And there's no sex involved either – well, not the sort you get dished up in some books and films these days. All that mauling and jumping into bed with each other every five minutes. It's hard at times to recognise a real story amongst it all! No, that's not for Clive and me, I know. Not that the subject has been broached even. There are far more important things to concern us, as you will understand. Don't get me wrong: it's not that I'm anti-sex or anything, but I've always believed in the right time and place for everything, and time alone will determine how things work out for us. Perhaps it's because we're older and – dare I say it? – wiser that we think as we do. It's all happened so quickly too. You can't just ignore it, pretend there's nothing there, because there is.

I don't know what Jim would think, I'm sure. I don't think he can comprehend very much about anything at present. There really isn't anything stopping Clive and me getting together when a decent time has elapsed after the tragedy of Esther's death. There is Jim, of course – I can't see all three of us living together somehow. There I go – getting ahead of myself again! We'll just have to wait and see what develops. All I'm sure about is I love Clive so much and he loves me. It takes some people months, even years, to develop a close relationship, but with Clive and me, well, it was a matter of weeks. It seemed to be upon us both before we knew it; it sort of took us by surprise, I think.

I had a very unsettled night last night. I was troubled by bad dreams. I kept going up lots of stairs, and just as I got to the top a door closed in my face. Then I'd try stairs going in another direction, only to find my way barred at the top of this flight by yet another door closing. I tried to open the door, but was unable to. It was as if I couldn't get anywhere, no matter how hard I tried. That sort of reflects my lifestyle I realised when

I sat down to think about it this morning. I found myself taking more headache tablets for I had yet another of my bad heads. It must be all the tension I've been feeling of late. There was Esther's death and how I was connected to that, my great attraction to Clive, and then the worry of Jim with his strange habits and moods. 'How will it all end up?' I wondered. Life seemed so much simpler before – before I got to know Clive, that is. Yes, simpler, but not so exciting. I can't imagine my life without knowing Clive now!

Chapter 20

"Oh, my dear, am I, or am I not, in a state of shock? Well, I am – I most certainly am. If it wasn't for that Clive next door I don't know what I should have done, and that's a fact. I don't like the man particularly – I mean, he's very secretive, isn't he? But after last night, well, I don't think he's so bad. It was like this, you see, dear: I was in bed, just dozing off, when it happened!"

"What happened?" I asked.

Yes, you've guessed – it was her again, Mrs Jackson!

"A man, my dear – some intruder must have got into my house. I always keep the small light on by my bed for if I've to get up in the night. As you may know, dear, I do have a bit of bladder trouble and need to go fairly often. Anyway, I looked and saw my bedroom door handle turn. What a fright that gave me! Then I heard a sort of heavy breathing and the handle went back to the closed position. Oh, I tell you, I was a nervous wreck! I got out of bed, put my dressing gown on and gingerly opened my bedroom door. I couldn't see anyone. I put the stairs light on. I keep an old poker near the top of the stairs, so I picked it up and shook it about, rattling the banisters as I went downstairs. I still didn't see anyone, so I went to Clive's house and banged on his door. I told him what I'd seen and heard. I was shaking so much I could hardly talk. Oh, my dear, it was the most dreadful experience!"

I thought she'd never stop for breath, but she did eventually. She followed me into the kitchen and sat down to take a short rest after her outburst.

"Was Clive on his own, then?" I asked.

"Well, of course he was. Who else would be there? She's not there any more, is she?"

"No, I suppose not," I said.

"I'll tell you what, dear: whoever it was who got into my house, well, he, or she, ran across the road in the dark and disappeared down the side of your house! Now, what do you think about that, eh?"

"Well, we heard no disturbance," I told her. "Maybe you heard a bit of a noise and you imagined someone was in your house. Our minds can play funny tricks on us at times – especially when we're tired," I suggested.

"Oh, I can see you don't believe me; and if you're going to be like that about it, I'm going!"

"Don't be offended – please don't go off in a huff. I just wondered how anyone could have got into your place when you've so many locks and bolts on all your doors and windows, that's all," I told her.

"Well, I'll tell you how. I accidentally left the back door unlocked. I've never done such a stupid thing before, so what do you say to that?" Mrs Jackson looked almost triumphant, like she'd just won a hand of cards over formidable opponents.

I began to be a little sorry I had made my former remarks about her imagining her 'intruder', as she seemed quite distraught, so I attempted to smooth troubled waters somewhat by saying, "Oh well, in that case someone could have got in."

"Not *could* have got in – *did* get in!" Mrs Jackson emphasised. "I tell you, the whole episode nearly finished me off! I've a good mind to sell up and go and live with my sister I'm so shaken up. If it hadn't been for that Clive I'd never have gone back into the house. He came in and searched everywhere till he was sure it was safe for me to return. He was most helpful really – especially as he is in the middle of all his own troubles. I've just had a thought too," she said.

"What's that?" I asked curiously.

"Well, you know how somebody broke into Clive's house and did that appalling thing to his wife? It could have been the same one getting into my place! Oh, my God, it doesn't bear thinking about. I'm going, dear. I feel quite weak. I must get back for my nerve tablets. Bye, dear. Oh my, I do feel bad!"

And she was gone once again.

Well, at least I know now for sure Mrs Jackson didn't know I was behind the door in Clive's house when she called on him for help. And she didn't know it was me running back to my house.

Move, did she say? To live with her sister? I can't see her doing that. She once told me they can't agree with each other for more than five minutes at a time. They fight like cat and dog! She's said before that she'll pack up and go to live with her sister, but it's never materialised. She might just go, but I very much doubt it.

I got to thinking today that if it's *Mrs* Jackson, then there must have been a Mr Jackson at some stage, though I've never heard it mentioned round here. I've only been in her house once or twice and, now I come to think of it, I didn't see any photos in there or anything to suggest there once was a Mr Jackson. I've tried broaching the subject with her on a few occasions, but I never get any satisfaction. She either goes quiet and stiff-lipped and looks offended or she gabbles on at twice her normal speed, changing the subject.

Mrs Jackson is extremely good at getting to know everybody's business, down to the last detail; but she's very careful not to reveal hers, except the bits she wants others to know which give her great personal satisfaction. For example, she was interviewed by our local paper when they opened the brand-new Co-op store in town and she'd bought a raffle ticket there and won a year's free groceries. Oh, she never misses a chance to bring that one up!

You know, I find it hard to believe that anyone got into Mrs Jackson's house. I half think she imagined it. She's a bit like that. If she thinks she's not getting much attention she'll invent something so she does get it! She's come over to my place at times with the most far-fetched stories I've ever heard. I've gone along and humoured her in her imaginings usually. I have an advantage over most people there, as I've become so used to humouring Jim in his hallucinations and strange ways over the years.

I've just seen a police car outside Mrs Jackson's. She must have contacted them about her so-called intruder. I expect they'll be looking for fingerprints and so on.

Chapter 21

There's been great activity in our house these past two weeks. Jim's been working feverishly on coffin number two. I don't know what the rush is for, I'm sure. It's had one advantage: it's given Jim an appetite and he's eaten up nearly everything I've prepared for him whilst he's been so busy. What he consumed in the few weeks before that wouldn't have fed a bird, I tell you.

I got a shock tonight when I took Jim's meal up to him. I couldn't find him at first. I saw the spare-room door was open a little. I looked in. I became aware of a slight breathing sound behind me. I turned round just in time to see the lid of the coffin being raised and a hand on the side of the lid. It was Jim's hand. He sat up in the box and carefully lifted the lid off and placed it on the floor.

He gave me that weird half-smile again and said, "It's good, Martha – a good fit!"

And then he climbed out, replacing the lid.

I made no comment myself, but went to his room, leaving his tray on the table as usual. I wish Jim would get rid of this preoccupation with death – it's most unnatural.

A parcel came for Jim today – a sort of square-shaped box and fairly heavy too. I can't imagine who'd be sending Jim a parcel. I've not known him to get even a letter for years. Well, he wouldn't, would he, when he supposedly died years ago! He never sees anybody and nobody sees him

– well, apart from me, that is. I had half a mind not to give Jim the parcel at all – just open it myself and see what it was. I think curiosity got the better of me in that direction though. I was even more curious to see Jim's reaction when I gave him the parcel and how he would behave when he opened it. So this is what I did. It all proved a bit disappointing, for there was very little reaction from Jim. He took out his penknife and prised open the top of the box and took out several smaller cardboard boxes and only looked in one or two.

He muttered to himself that "They will do very nicely," and then he picked up a wooden cross he was carving and ignored his parcel.

"Who sent your parcel, Jim?" I asked.

"Tool shop," he said simply. "I wrote off for it. That's what I wanted the pen and paper for," he said.

'My,' I thought, 'that was a long time ago.' But how did he get it posted? I know I didn't post it. Then who did? Jim? Surely not. He never ventures downstairs, let alone go out of the house! It's just struck me that with Jim's burst of activity lately with his woodwork his speech seems to have improved dramatically. There's very little incoherent muttering at present. I suppose I ought to be pleased about that, but all I feel lately is uneasy about Jim. There's some kind of change I can't account for.

It was next day I found out how Jim had got his letter posted. He'd evidently thrown it out of the window in his room and a neighbour of mine had picked it up and posted it thinking I must have dropped it on my way out to go shopping.

A few days later I was waiting at the bus stop, chatting to a neighbour from three doors up from me. It was Mrs Brown, who'd lived in her house for fifty-seven years, she told me – ever since the street was built. She also told me about picking a letter up and posting it a few days ago. She thought maybe I'd dropped it as it was by my front gate. I told a white lie and said it was my letter, and I thanked her for her kindness. Well, strictly speaking, it was Jim's letter, but no matter. I was thinking to myself that my Jim certainly can spring some surprises!

The bombshell came next day when I took Jim his evening meal.

"I want to see him," he said.

"See him? See who, Jim?" I asked, bewildered.

"Him across the road – Clive. That's his name, isn't it? You should know if anybody should," Jim almost shouted.

It took my breath away for a few seconds. We'd lived in this house for ten years and Jim had never asked to see anybody but me. And now this. Whatever had moved him to ask such a thing? I decided on my plan of action. I mustn't appear disturbed at Jim's request – at least not unreasonably so, though I certainly felt it. If he'd asked to see Mrs Jackson or any of the near neighbours I wouldn't have cared, but Clive! And yet why should I be so perturbed? It wasn't as if I was married to Jim. He'd no claim on me that way, I know. Nevertheless Jim has regarded me more or less as his property all these years, and it could cause problems. But then, Jim could hardly be aware that Clive and I have a strong and growing relationship going on, could he? Whatever was the case, I felt extremely uneasy when I heard Jim's request.

"Well, are you going to ask him over to see me or not?" Jim asked almost impatiently.

"Yes, Jim, if that's what you want, but you've never wanted to see anybody all these years; you've only wanted me here," I told him.

"Exactly, but that was before I lost you," Jim said.

"Lost me? I haven't gone away. Whatever do you mean by that, Jim?"

Did Jim mean he'd lost me to Clive? No, how could he? He knew nothing about that side of things. Then what did he mean?

I tried to bluff my way out of it, saying, "Oh, I understand, Jim – you mean I've been paying a bit of attention across the road to that man there and you shouted for me and I wasn't there. Yes, that's it, Jim. I wasn't lost at all. You're right, Jim: I have been over the road once or twice lately to offer Clive a few words of sympathy. After all, he's in the middle of a very sad time indeed, losing his wife."

I thought this explanation should satisfy Jim for the time being. I'd told Jim very little about the 'murder', but I expect he'd heard snippets from Mrs Jackson when she'd popped over here to see me. She has a rather loud voice!

"Yes," said Jim, "he's lost her and I've lost you."

"Don't be silly, Jim – I'm not lost. I'm here. Look at me – Martha, your Martha."

His eyes glazed over for a few seconds as if what I'd been saying hadn't registered at all.

Then he spoke very quietly: "Yes, I did know a Martha once. You're a bit like her, you know, but she's gone now." And he fell to weeping fitfully. He hadn't done that for a long time.

I left him for a few minutes, then went back to his room.

"Look, Jim – I'll ask the man across the road – I'll ask Clive to come and see you as soon as I can. They're burying his wife tomorrow, so we'd better leave it for a day or so."

Jim began to laugh louder and louder, but when he stopped and turned his face towards me two large tears rolled down his cheeks. He didn't say any more. I left the room.

I'd better get over to Clive's this evening and tell him what Jim's been asking. I don't know what Clive will think about that.

Jim's been working again this afternoon, knocking and banging up there. He seems to have pulled himself together a bit now. Perhaps he'll forget about wanting to see Clive, after all. I took him his meal tonight as usual. He looked tired. He'd been working most of the day on his 'project', as he calls it nowadays.

I actually watched him take his sleeping tablets tonight, so I know he'll be settled till morning. Half an hour later he was in bed fast asleep.

"Right," I thought, "I'll go and see Clive now."

Chapter 22

Clive had someone in with him when I went over, so this threw me a little.

"No, no, come in, Martha – meet my brother David," Clive said.

I went in. I hesitated in the hallway awkwardly for a moment then I recovered my composure and went in the lounge. Clive introduced me.

"Pleased to meet you, David," I said.

"Likewise, I'm sure," said Clive's brother brightly.

"I don't wish to intrude, Clive. I just came over to, er . . ." I stammered.

"Don't be silly! You're not intruding at all, Martha. David's up from London for the funeral. He's staying with me till it's all over. Funny we hardly see one another nowadays. David's mostly abroad on business," Clive said.

"Yes, Clive's right there. We haven't met up for a long time. I couldn't get back from abroad even for Brian's funeral, and now there's Esther! Terrible tragedy – just terrible!" David said.

There were a few seconds of awkward silence and it was Clive who broke it: "I've been telling David all about you, Martha, haven't I, David?"

"You certainly have – all good, of course. Clive is so grateful for your help at this tragic time, I know."

"I've done very little really."

"That's not what I've heard. Clive says you've been a tower of strength."

"I don't know what to say to that."

I mumbled something and David handed me a drink. He said it was a Martini. I'd never had such a thing before, but it tasted quite pleasant.

"I forgot the ice, Martha. I'm sure you would like some." And he dropped three pieces into my glass.

A cold shiver went through me at the mention of ice in that house!

I could see that David was quite a different character from Clive. He seemed much more outgoing and confident and used to meeting people.

"Yes," he said, "Clive is going through a hellish bad time at the moment – two deaths within such a short space of time. It's fortunate that Clive has you to talk to, Martha, for he's a pretty introverted guy, as I suppose you've found out for yourself. Never could make the first move, could you, Clive?"

"No, I haven't got your gift for that kind of thing, certainly," Clive replied.

"So it is all the more surprising that Clive has managed to make your acquaintance, Martha!"

"I don't find Clive hard to talk to at all," I said. "On the contrary, I find him an interesting and approachable person."

That seemed to close that topic of conversation – for several seconds at least. I was trying hard to weigh up how much David knew about Clive and me, whether Clive had mentioned anything about our relationship, but David, if he knew anything, gave away very little.

"I was just saying to Clive, Martha, before you arrived, I was asking him what the hell are the police doing about it all? About the break-in, and about what happened to poor Esther. As far as I can judge, they don't seem to have got very far!" David said.

"To be fair," I said, "I do think they are doing their best. They've carried out endless enquiries and chased up even the remotest clues they thought might be of significance. What else can we expect of them?"

"What else? What else? I'll tell you what else: they should have got the person or persons responsible by now! It sticks out a mile that the intruders, or intruder, must have done it – murdered Esther, then her body was dumped in the freezer! I'd kill them myself if I could lay hands on whoever did it!"

David had worked himself up into a real frenzy by this time.

"Steady on there, David" Clive said. "Getting upset like that won't do any of us any good. As you say, we've had, and are having, a horrible time and we need all the support we can get. Martha has been invaluable in providing that and I can't thank her enough."

"Please, Clive, I've done little. I wish I could have done more."

David topped our glasses up. I wasn't accustomed to drinking much alcohol, but I quite enjoyed it.

David finished his drink in one and then said, "I'm sorry, folks, for my little outburst earlier, but I do get so furious thinking that the police haven't made much progress as yet. Anyway, let's change the subject. How about the three of us going into town for a meal? I don't know about you, Martha, but Clive and I haven't had a proper meal since yesterday. Will you join us, Martha? It would be an opportunity for me to show a little appreciation for all the help you've given Clive."

"It's a bit late for me, thank you, David, and I can't leave Jim for long. I don't expect Clive's told you I have Jim to look after. Mind you, Jim was fast asleep when I came over here. He has to take sleeping tablets every night. He should sleep soundly till morning. Yes, I suppose I could go out for a meal. Why not?"

I addressed most of what I said to David.

"Wonderful – that's settled," he said.

"Just give me ten minutes to change into something more suitable," I said.

"Nonsense – you look just fine as you are, Martha," Clive told me.

Actually, I didn't look too bad in my navy two-piece so I agreed to stay as I was.

"Well, there you are, then. Your husband will be all right, I'm certain. He'll never realise you've been out, Martha," David assured me.

"Oh, er, he's not my husband. He's just . . . Well, all that would take too long to explain," I said.

Ten minutes later we were in David's Mercedes speeding off down the road. I'd never travelled in such a posh car before! That must have given Mrs Jackson something to think about as she saw us go. She was behind her net curtains again – her favourite spot in her house, I'm beginning to think.

We had an enjoyable meal in an Indian restaurant just off the High Street. I certainly hadn't been there before. With Jim as he'd been all these years, I seldom got the chance to socialise, so it was all the more a treat for me. Even when Jim had his full faculties he never would try any of 'that foreign muck', as he called Indian, Chinese or any other food served in restaurants which he didn't consider to be strictly English.

I think the visit to the restaurant served to give some sense of relief to Clive and David, and even to me, midst the sadness and worry brought on by recent events. And I was very much aware we were far from out of the woods yet!

It was after one thirty when I got to bed. I had peeped in on Jim and he was dead to the world, as I'd expected he would be. There were bits of cut electrical wires on the floor by his bed, so I guessed he had been working earlier in the evening on something or other before I went out. Or had he been working again whilst I was out? No – I think there were bits of wire about before I went out, weren't there? I couldn't be sure. No matter now. I was suddenly very tired. I went to sleep that night feeling more satisfied than I had done for some time.

Chapter 23

When I awoke it was to hear activity from the spare room. I slipped on my dressing gown and went to see what was going on, and there he was, Jim, working away busily. It's funny he doesn't lock himself in the spare room any more when he's 'working' – or lock me out, for that matter. The only time Jim seemed happy was when he was doing his little jobs in there.

I was quite astonished at what I saw, for Jim's 'work' was all but completed: a coffin that anyone would be proud of. The box was finished and gleamed in the morning sunlight pouring through the window. The brass handles were in place, reflecting the sun's rays like laser beams. The angle at which the coffin was set as you entered the room made it look a lot longer than it actually was, just like those pictures you see in glossy magazines of new cars which give the illusion that they are like Cadillacs when in reality they are more like Minis! I could see several wired circuits fastened at intervals near the top edges of the coffin. Was he thinking of illuminating it? It wouldn't surprise me. Just another slant on his lunacy, I guess.

He didn't appear to notice me at first, then he almost jumped, accompanied by nervous twitches when he faced me full on.

"Don't work too hard, Jim," I said. "You'll tire yourself out."

"There's not much time," he muttered. "Not much time."

And he slunk past me and went into his room.

I had a phone call from my sister today. She wondered why I'd never replied to her letter. She's just had the phone put in, it seems. She said that as I appeared to have lost the ability to write to her, the next best thing was to get the phone put in so we can 'correspond' that way. She always was the sarcastic one. She's very good in lots of other ways though. She'd help anyone in trouble. She rang me really to say she's going on a Women's Institute holiday next week – a tour of Holland and Belgium for fifteen days and reasonably priced. She's been a member of the WI for years. She's been in just about every class they hold: needlework, household repairs, upholstery, cookery . . . You name it, she's done it!

I'm very glad for her that she's going on holiday. I know she'd like to come to stay with me, or have me stay with her, but, as you may guess, Jim's the big problem. This will be a real holiday for Ruth, and I hope she thoroughly enjoys herself.

Chapter 24

It's Esther's funeral today. I wonder how Clive is feeling. Pretty dreadful, I should think. I hope he doesn't break down and maybe say something he shouldn't. He could blurt it all out at the graveside, confessing to what he did. He's so honest at the bottom of him. I shan't be there either to give him support. Well, it wouldn't be wise, would it? I only hope it gets over quickly.

It's ten fifteen now – they must be on their way to the cemetery. There'll only be Clive and his brother there, I believe, and the priest. Esther's relatives opted not to attend, circumstances being as they are. A private memorial service is to be held at a later date in the village church where Esther hailed from. I actually said a private prayer for the repose of her soul. I hope her spirit is at rest and that she doesn't bear too great ill-will towards Clive. I'm not at all sure that you can bear ill-will towards anyone when you're dead, but there it is.

I don't think she was a happy person when she was alive – all that shouting and harassment she poured out on Clive daily. There was certainly something very lacking in that marriage. It could almost have been a cry for help on Esther's part. If Clive is to blame at all in this instance, I think it is because he was too tolerant over the years. That can be as big a mistake as being overbearing. That's how I see it, as an outsider. I'm tolerant with Jim to a degree, but I do take a firm stand on certain issues; and Jim, although he's not always in his right mind, is well aware of how far he can go!

***

It'll be over now – well over. It's after one o'clock. I've been keeping an eye out, but so far I haven't seen Clive or his brother return. That car of David's is quite an eye-catcher! It sort of reflects him with his outgoing, dynamic personality. I don't know exactly what he does for a living, but he doesn't seem short of a bob or two. I believe he was married at one time, but it didn't last evidently and there was no issue from the union.

I often wonder how Esther came to be wheelchair-bound. Clive has never explained it. Perhaps one day he will. I imagine it will take him a long, long time to come to terms with this tragedy in his life – if, in fact, he ever does. Me too, for that matter. I'm quite heavily involved myself, aren't I?

It's a poor day for weather today – intermittent rain – and it doesn't seem to have been properly light since dawn broke. A fitting background to the gloom surrounding a funeral. I've only been to a few funerals in my life, and on each occasion it poured down. At Jim's 'funeral' the air was suddenly rent by ear-splitting thunderclaps and forked lightning, as if the Almighty was voicing His objection at the mock interment! I've had to put the light on. I could hardly see to read the paper.

Oh my! It's here in the 'Stop Press': 'Funeral today of Esther Morton, disabled woman, found murdered in freezer.'

'My God! Hardly an epitaph anyone would want to be remembered by,' I thought.

***

I took Jim's meal up a bit earlier tonight. It was lamb chops, roast potatoes, peas and cauliflower – a meal he loves, as a rule. He must have eaten more lamb chops than anybody I know. That's when he was in a good eating mood, of course. But, as I said a little while ago, Jim is on a high at the moment as regards his eating habits. I do believe he's putting on a few pounds too.

I've just had a cup of tea and a biscuit myself. I can't settle to eating today. I can't stop thinking about that Indian meal I had. I've had disturbing tummy rumblings all day. I'm just not used to that kind of food and its strong spices, although I love the flavours.

When I went up to collect Jim's tray I was pleased to see he'd eaten all his meal.

I was just about to ask him if he'd enjoyed it when he said, "Well, when's he coming to see me, eh?"

"When's who coming to see you, Jim?" I said, although I knew the answer already.

"Clive. Clive – him over the road. What did he say?" Jim asked.

"I haven't had a chance to ask him properly yet, Jim" I said.

"Haven't asked him? You're always over there – what for, I don't know."

"Listen, Jim – I've only gone over there to see if I can help in any way. You ought to be ashamed of yourself begrudging help to anyone in need. Now, just you think about it and don't be so selfish," I said angrily.

Jim sat in silence for a time and sulked.

Then he said, "I know what you're up to, Martha. You're a Jezebel, you are. You're trying to get me to marry you, aren't you? You're disgusting when you're married already!"

"What on earth are you talking about, Jim? Are you mad?" I said, and immediately I was sorry I'd made that remark. After all, he had been certified insane all those years ago, hadn't he?

"No, Martha, I'm not mad, but your husband is and you haven't been faithful to him. You've taken advantage of him all these years. I saw him over the road out of my window. He's staying with that Clive, isn't he?"

"You mean David?" I said.

"Yes, David, if that's what they call him – your husband. You've been keen enough to take his money all these years. He thought you'd go back to him some day, but you haven't, have you? Well, scheme as much as you like, but I'll never marry you, Martha – never. So there!"

What a muddled mind Jim has, thinking I was married to David. He also evidently thought I wanted to get him, Jim, to marry me! Well, here was a turn-up for the books! However he got all that into his head I'll never know. His mind's in a worse mix-up than ever. But the strange thing is that his speech has improved out of all recognition. I wonder what is the explanation for that?

"Jim, listen to me: you don't know what you're saying. You've got things all mixed up. But forget that for the moment. I will ask Clive to come and see you if that's what you want. He buried his wife today, so just wait a day or so, Jim."

"Do what you want – it won't matter soon, anyway." Jim said, and what he meant by that I don't know. He's had this thing about time being short lately. "Just remember this, Martha, when you're making these wicked plans: you reap what you sow. Mark my words: you reap what you sow. Think before it's too late!" And Jim said this almost threateningly.

I picked up his tray and went downstairs.

***

It was late when I got up next morning. I'd slept heavily and got up at least an hour beyond my usual time. I'd been troubled again by unpleasant dreams. I've just seen the curtains pulled back across the road. Clive and David must have returned either very late last night or very early this morning. I see the Mercedes is in the driveway. I'll go over there later and see how things went yesterday. I'll ask Clive too about coming to see Jim.

Chapter 25

"Martha, Martha, you there, dear?"

It was Mrs Jackson, in by the back door again. I did promise myself I'd keep that door bolted so she couldn't surprise me as she's just done now. Too late – here she comes.

"Ah, there you are, dear. My, you're usually up and dressed by this time, but here you are still in your dressing gown! Naughty, naughty!" she said.

Oh, I did hate it when she talked to me like that, but I always tried to hide the fact.

"No, no, Mrs Jackson, I'm fine – just thought I'd get up leisurely for a change," I said.

"And why not indeed? But listen, dear, and I'll tell you the real reason I'm here. It's about the funeral, you see. What a day, with such awful weather too! Oh, quite moving it was though. There weren't many there, which surprised me – just Clive and his brother. You know, the one with the Lamborghini."

"Actually, Mrs Jackson, it's a Mercedes," I interrupted.

"Ooh, fancy you knowing that! But then, you were out in it with them the other evening, weren't you? Go anywhere nice, did you? Well, I don't blame you, dear. I mean, you haven't got much going for you, have you?" She asked.

I couldn't get over the fact that Mrs Jackson had actually gone to the funeral! I didn't think even she would do that, taking into account the circumstances. But then, I shouldn't be surprised at anything she might do.

"How is, er, he, dear? Mad as ever, I expect. Well, I suppose he can't help it, as you once said, but you really should have him put away, dear. It's all too much for you. I know you don't like me saying that, and I'm sorry, but I'm only thinking of you, dear. But where was I? Oh yes, the funeral yesterday. Well, there were one or two reporters there from the local press, you know, and somebody was taking pictures – rather bad taste, I thought. But of course it was no ordinary death, was it, so I suppose we should expect that sort of thing. There were a couple of plain-clothed policemen there too – watching for the murderer to return to the scene of the crime, eh? But of course we know the real scene of the crime was next door to me, don't we, dear? Oh my, I still don't know if I can go on living there after all this. Oh, I nearly forgot: the flowers were beautiful. I thought ours from the neighbours were the best. There were only a couple of other wreaths there, anyway – probably from Clive and his brother. I'm glad I went, anyway – did my bit, as it were. I think I got into some of the pictures that were taken. I could be in the papers or even on the news! I thought you might have been there, dear – you know, with you seeing to his wife and all that when he was away," she chuntered on.

"No, I think Clive wanted it all as quiet as possible. Just he and his brother were all he expected to be there, but it seems it didn't work out that way," I told her.

"Yes, but you have to remember, dear, it was no ordinary funeral so it was bound to cause a bit of a stir. It's not every day you get a murder on your road – not that anybody would want that, but I mean . . . Anyway, I just wanted you to know it all went off as well as could be expected in the circumstances. Must fly, dear – I've got the washing to start on. Bye, dear."

And she was gone, once more, out of the back door. Trust her to go to the funeral!

I pottered round for the rest of the morning, starting on a number of household tasks and completing none. It wasn't like me to be disorganised, as Jim used to note many times. He said I was a creature of habit. I have set routines for almost everything and I stick to them rigidly. Well, I did, that is, until recently – until Clive, I suppose. He's responsible for a whole lot of changes in my life – undreamed-of changes, as I've begun to realise. I know I've become a changed person since meeting Clive. I used to be satisfied with my lot.

When I was at school some of the kids called me Mouse because I was so quiet and introverted, but I'm not now. Clive awakened strong emotions in me I'd never experienced before – strong feelings that cannot be ignored. I feel an undeniable compulsion to follow them wherever they might lead me. I've begun to develop a 'throw caution to the winds' attitude – not a bit like me really.

It has never been my way to take risks over anything – till now. And yet in all this there is always an air of hesitation, an apprehension of what might be the outcome if I give way to my desires completely. It is like warring factions within me, a game of tug of war, my old self and my new self in combat. Which will be the victor? I wonder.

I was trying to figure out why I felt so dizzy as I stood up. Then I realised I hadn't had anything to eat hardly since that Indian meal with Clive and David. I'd been about to make a cup of tea when Mrs Jackson made her appearance. So I made one now and some beef sandwiches, which used up all the meat from the joint I roasted for Jim the other day. There was quite a plateful. I went upstairs with a couple for Jim, but he didn't want any. I decided to take the sandwiches over to Clive and David – maybe they'd like a bite.

I was right. They were appreciative of the eats and dived in voraciously. David made a pot of tea. Clive looked very strained and I told him so.

"I'm all right," he said.

David must have heard what I said, and as he brought in the tea he said, "You know, Martha, Clive bore up remarkably well, but what got me was those stupid sightseers. I can't imagine what it was they expected to see. That nosey bitch from next door was the worst. She seemed to think she was witnessing some kind of entertainment. Just came along to gawp and nose, that's all. God, how I hate people like that!"

"Don't go on so, David. I don't suppose my neighbour can help herself. I'm sure she means well really," Clive said.

"Oh, Clive, how can you say that? You don't surely believe it? You told me yourself only this morning that Mrs Jackson just can't resist minding other people's business. She knows what's going on round here about most people, I imagine," I said.

Clive declined further comment.

It was me who started the conversation off again: "Let's leave Mrs Jackson out of it for the moment. I'm sure you're both relieved the funeral is over."

"You can say that again," said David, "but I won't rest until they find the bastard who murdered Esther. And for what? God knows Clive hasn't found much missing, so why was she killed?"

"Stop it, David. I can't take much more right now," Clive said.

"I'm sorry, Clive, but this terrible death makes me so very angry. What a terrible waste of a life! I think we could all do with a drink."

"But we've just had tea," I said.

"No, a proper drink. I'll get some."

And off David went in search of refreshment. Clive and I were left alone for a few moments.

"Oh, Clive," I said as we comforted one another in a light embrace. "Oh, Clive, I've been so worried about you. I'm glad Esther has gone to her rest for both our sakes. It's over."

"Is it over? I wonder, Martha," Clive whispered. "But—"

"Sh! David is coming with the drinks," I said, and I moved away from Clive to sit a short distance from him.

"Here you are, Martha – a sherry. Is that OK?"

"Fine, thank you, David."

He gave Clive a whisky and had one himself.

"Cheers, everybody! To better days," David said, and Clive and I certainly seconded that!

"Oh, Clive, I nearly forgot. It's Jim. He's been asking if you'll come to see him sometime. Don't ask me why. He's never wanted to see anyone but me all these ten years so far. You must be special. Would you do that – come and see Jim when you feel able?"

"I'll be glad to see him if that's what he wants. Ask him when, Martha," Clive said.

"I will. Thanks Clive."

"Another drink, you two?" David asked.

"Not for me, thanks, David," I said. "I'd better get back home. Thanks all the same."

"Just a minute, Martha – why don't you come out with us again for a meal tonight?" David asked. "I know we all enjoyed each other's company last time we went, and it might be my last chance. I've to be on my way again soon – to India this time."

"Sorry, David – I must decline on this occasion. It's Jim, you see. I don't feel I can leave him for too long at present. I've got a strange feeling he's up to something; so I'd rather not, if you don't mind. It would take too long to explain all about Jim's problems though. Clive knows about my situation. But you and Clive must certainly go out. It seems you see one another so seldom these days, so take advantage while you can," I said.

"Yes, Martha, we will. I'll ring for a table somewhere. Oh, damn! I forgot you've no phone, Clive."

David seemed somewhat frustrated. He wasn't used to people who lacked even the simplest mod cons like a telephone.

"I'll ring from my house," I said. "What time and where?"

"About eight would be nice, and at the same place we went last time. Are you sure you don't mind, Martha?" David enquired.

"Consider it done."

"Thanks, Martha."

David gave me a peck on the cheek. I smiled at them both and left.

As soon as I got home I booked the meal for Clive and David. I did feel the slightest disappointment that I wouldn't be joining them.

Chapter 26

I was tidying a few bits up in my kitchen when my phone rang, but by the time I picked it up the ringing had stopped. I can't think who that was. It wouldn't have been my sister – she's away on holiday. I get very few calls indeed and I don't make many myself. Jim's never used the phone. He doesn't seem aware of its existence. Anyway, it's downstairs in the hall and he never ventures down there, does he? If anyone knocks at the door when I am out there's no one to answer it – certainly not Jim. It's not surprising that many neighbours think I live alone. Of course those in contact with Mrs Jackson will know different.

I looked in on Jim: fast asleep. I didn't expect anything different. Those double-strength sleeping pills are most effective, I must say, and I always watch him take them now. He's usually asleep for a good twelve hours with those. You wouldn't think, to look at him when he's asleep, there is anything wrong with him. I've often wondered how things would be if we'd actually got married as planned and if Jim's mind had remained intact. Maybe we'd have had a child. I know I was thirty-six when we were to have married, but I could possibly have had one or two children by now. Perhaps it's just as well I haven't. What if Jim's mind had gone after we were married? What then? And if we'd had a child, it would have been worse. I might have thought I was to blame as well. No, if it had to happen, it's best Jim's mind went when it did.

And then there's Clive now to be considered. Maybe if Jim and I had married there'd still have been Clive. Who can tell? How can you forecast what you're going to feel about someone in time to come? You can't. You're not in control of it – it's in control of you, it seems to me, whatever *it* is.

When I've heard of people in such a situation I've thought, 'Silly things! Why don't they pull themselves together instead of being so ridiculous?' But I don't think that now – no, not since I've experienced it myself with Clive.

I don't know why I should feel any guilt, really. As I've said before, I'm not married to Jim; I'm not married to anybody. I'm a free agent as far as that goes. I can marry or not as I wish. Oh, I know what you're thinking: what about Jim? Who'd look after him? Well, don't worry yourselves on that account – I'll never abandon him. I'll see him all right. I feel I still owe him that at least.

***

I had a card from my sister today, from Holland. She certainly seems to be enjoying her holiday there. The weather sounds favourable too. I showed it to Jim. All he said was he wasn't interested in what 'his sister' was doing any more since she never bothered coming to see him. No good telling him it's really my sister who sent the card. Funny thing is he hasn't got a sister – never has had a sister! Why he should think he has one now I don't know.

He never wants me to sit with him in the evenings nowadays – told me so in no uncertain terms! Once I've delivered his evening meal to him he as good as dismisses me. I have tried staying a while, but he hardly speaks; he just sits there staring straight ahead of him. He's in a world of his own. One side of his mouth has started to droop when he gives his half-smile. I don't know what he's smiling about. It's as if he sees something I can't.

I saw in the paper today that the police are holding two men for questioning in connection with break-ins in this area – including the one at Clive's, it seems! A sudden twinge of conscience struck me as I read this. How awful it would be if it was proved somehow that one or both of these men were responsible for the killing of Clive's wife! The police seem certain now, for reasons best known to them, that two persons broke into Clive's house on that fateful night, and maybe they committed the murder.

I keep thinking, 'What if those the police suspect at present are by some means or other found guilty of Esther's murder? How could Clive and I ever live with such an injustice, knowing the truth of what really did happen! Knowing who did kill Esther! KILL - a horrible, horrible word! The man I have fallen in love with is a murderer! When I think of it like that I feel sick - dear, gentle, unassuming Clive. And yet he is a murderer in the eyes of the world - or rather he will be if it all comes to light, which God forbid! But to me Clive is a dear man who has been broken down in spirit and who has acted absolutely out of character under extreme provocation, the strain of which built up over the years until he could stand no more. And in one awful moment he snapped, like an elastic band stretched too far!

I almost imagine myself in court putting this as a plea to the counsel for the defence. Would a jury be moved by it? I wonder. No, all this business is a long way from over. Perhaps it is only just the beginning. Maybe it is only a dream I had that Clive and I will find lasting happiness one day. The horrific events of the recent past are surely a poor basis on which to build something good and lasting.

Chapter 27

I had to call in an electrician this afternoon. First the twin-tub broke down, then the iron stopped working after it gave a terrific bang and a blue flash came from where the flex fits into the base. Then the cooker did the same and the downstairs lights wouldn't work. Such a thing has never happened before. I admit I'm a bit afraid of things electrical. Mrs Jackson is always trying to persuade me to get an electric lawnmower, but I can never bring myself to do it. Well, you do hear of people electrocuting themselves by accident.

The electricity people were very quick when I rang with my worries: a man came out within the hour. I stressed on the phone that the matter was extremely urgent. The electrician went round all the sockets and wiring and did a thorough check in the electric cupboard. It took him the best part of an hour and I saw he's replaced some wiring and sockets. He was wanting to go upstairs, but I made some excuse about someone up there with a contagious illness and he didn't press the point. He fixed all the appliances that had gone wrong and said they were now fine. I told him the lights were OK upstairs anyway, though I didn't know if that was the case! But no way was he going up there! What sort of a place would he have thought it with two coffins in a room upstairs? I found out later that the lights do work upstairs, thank goodness! The workman kept mentioning about the electric system being overloaded, or some such thing, but I'm afraid that doesn't mean much to me. I took his word for it and he went. He did say that in his opinion the whole house needs rewiring and that I shouldn't leave it much longer before having it seen to. I'll have to consider that one very carefully!

Jim's been going quite mad lately – not mad insane, but mad meaning he's been busy working almost frantically to finish his caskets in the spare room. He has his two coffins sitting there side by side. I must say he's done an excellent job – if you like that sort of thing, that is. He's fixed up all sorts of wiring with small light bulbs inside the lids and round the bases. He's made as arrangement of a multi-plug system which fits in the light sockets – wires everywhere! I only hope it's safe and doesn't cause a fire! I'm going to try to persuade Jim to turn his talents to making something more normal, like a little table. I could do with one in the hallway.

Jim spoke to me a bit this evening when I gave him his meal.

"I can have a long rest now, Maggie," he said.

I noticed he'd gone back to calling me Maggie, instead of Martha, but I didn't remark on it.

"Of course you can have a rest now, Jim. You deserve it, you've worked so hard," I said.

"Who was that man who came here today, Maggie? I heard him talking," Jim said.

"Oh, that was the electrician, Jim. Some of the electrics went off and I was very worried."

At this Jim threw back his head and roared with laughter, louder than I had ever heard him laugh before. "But he didn't know, did he? He didn't find out, Maggie. No – I was too clever for him, that's why," Jim said, and he gave another great roar.

"Didn't find out what, Jim? Tell me."

"Oh, never you mind, Maggie. You'll find out soon enough," said Jim, and he seemed extremely pleased with himself about something.

And that was when it dawned on me that it must have been caused by all his wiring and lighting – 'overloading' was the word the electrician used. Well, maybe Jim was responsible for doing that with his peculiar wiring and such. I wouldn't be a bit surprised. I'll have to tell him to leave his wiring jobs alone if this is what comes of it.

As I went downstairs I was relieved to see the lights upstairs were working. If they had failed before, then the electrician must have fixed them from the electric cupboard downstairs.

Chapter 28

I was in town today, in the market. I bought my usual fruit and vegetables, and I had a few other things to buy for Jim. He'd made a short list. As I read it I saw 'shaving cream', 'mints' and – oh no! – more electrical stuff and 'bulbs'. Well, I'm certainly not having any more of that in the house, not after the recent trouble with the electrician. I decided to make some excuse up and tell Jim I couldn't get them.

I looked at my watch: ten to three. Time for a coffee. I went in the café opposite – the one I'd first gone in with Clive a long time ago. He was sitting there when I went in. We'd been doing this for a few weeks now, going out shopping on the same day and meeting up in the café. I just had coffee – I didn't want anything else. Food has interested me very little over the last day or two.

Clive told me his brother had left for India quite suddenly and he'd asked Clive to make his apologies to me for not saying goodbye. Clive said David was always off somewhere round the world on business. Yes, David certainly is very different from his brother – very different indeed. I suppose some women would find David extremely attractive. He has charm all right. I expect that's how he's got on so well in his business life. But I could never take to him in any other way than looking on him as an entertaining companion. Clive was much more than that to me, I knew.

"Penny for them," Clive said.

"Oh, nothing really. I'm just thinking how pleasant it is to be sitting here drinking coffee, that's all."

"It doesn't take much to please you, Martha, does it? Easily satisfied you are, my dear," Clive remarked.

"I suppose I am most of the time. Clive, did you see in the paper they've got someone, or maybe more than one, for questioning about the break-ins round our area?"

"Yes, I did. I actually had the police round again, Martha, asking all sorts of questions, and there was one bit of good news: they told me they're pretty confident of closing the case soon as regards Esther's death."

"Oh, my God, Clive, that's terrible!" I said.

"What do you mean, Martha, terrible? I think it's very good news – to have the awful business officially over. We'll be free – free of all guilt!"

"Stop it! Stop it, Clive! That's just what we won't be; we can't ever be free of the guilt," I said, and I burst into tears.

It took a couple of minutes before I had control of myself again. Clive put his arm round me to console me and gave me his handkerchief to wipe my eyes.

"Oh, Clive, it's just that if the police prove it's someone else, well, an innocent person would be punished for Esther's death. If that happens I couldn't live with you or myself in peace."

"Listen, Martha – we have to be sensible. Don't put a damper on our chance of happiness together by thinking such thoughts. The police are not yet certain who the guilty party, or parties, are. They've got to be 100 per cent sure before they charge anybody. No, they won't be able to prove anything definite, I'm certain – you'll see. It will be all right. The case will be left open pending further evidence, maybe for years, and there won't be any! No one will get hurt, Martha – don't worry so," Clive said, and he got up to pay the bill.

Unfortunately I'm not half so sure as Clive appears to be about how things will turn out.

We were on the bus going home when Clive asked, "Martha, didn't you say that your Jim wished to see me?"

"Oh yes, he did, but that was about a week ago and he hasn't mentioned it since. Don't worry – he's probably forgotten all about it by now. He's like that, you know, in his state of mind."

"But I'd like to see Jim – really I would, Martha. I'm quite curious," Clive said.

"You curious, Clive? I'd never have thought it – you're so reticent normally. You'll see a sick man if you do visit Jim – not physically, of course, but I do assure you that he is very sick mentally, very sick indeed!"

"It's strange, isn't it, Martha? You got to see Esther when no one else did; and maybe I'll see Jim, who never sees anyone but you," Clive said.

"True – true enough – but you're in for a shock. I'm warning you, Clive – wait till you see what he's spent months working on. I couldn't bring myself to tell you about it before!"

"What's that, then?" Clive enquired.

"You'll see. Just wait – you'll see!" I told him.

And he would!

"Sounds quite mysterious," Clive mused.

"You could say that, but tell me: when do you plan a visit?"

"I suppose there's no time like the present, so how about this evening if Jim's agreeable?" Clive suggested.

"I'd better see Jim first and see what sort of a mood he's in. I'll have to remind him he asked to see you. He can't handle shocks. You do realise, don't you, that I'm the only person Jim's seen and spoken to in the last ten years here?"

"You did tell me a little about this sometime ago, and I have to admit it's very strange behaviour indeed."

A minute later we were at our stop and we got off the bus together.

As we came abreast of my gate, Clive said, "I hope to see Jim this evening maybe?"

"Maybe. When I've spoken to Jim I'll let you know, Clive."

And I went up my drive. As I shut the front door I could see Mrs Jackson standing in her front garden – looking up at the sky, apparently. She'd been viewing us no doubt minutes before as we stood talking at my gate.

"All right, Jim, I've got your bits here – your shaving cream, mints and things. And I got you some beer," I said.

Jim said nothing and didn't even ask about the electrical stuff. I am quite relieved.

When I took Jim his meal this evening I broached the subject of Clive paying him a visit as requested.

"Clive, Clive, is he coming back? Is he alive, then?" asked Jim.

"What do you mean, Jim? Don't be silly – Clive's never been in here before to see you, so how could he be coming back? You do talk rubbish sometimes. Of course Clive's alive – I've just been talking to him. We were on the same bus coming from town," I said.

"No, Maggie, it's your mind – you're mixed up. I've been watching you, Maggie – you don't make any sense at times. You're unbalanced. To put it bluntly, my girl, I do believe your mind's going. You should see a doctor before it's too late! Maybe that would help you." And then he threw his head back and laughed with uncontrollable laughter just as he had done a day or so previously.

Him telling me I need to see a doctor because I am mixed up in my mind! Well, that's rich, that is! Really, what is coming over that man? I ask you! Then I realised I wouldn't get a satisfactory answer from Jim as to whether he wished to see Clive or not.

'Oh, forget it,' I told myself. 'It'll only cause a lot more trouble, I expect – to all of us.

Chapter 29

I waited till it got dark before I went over the road, mostly because I can't stand Mrs Jackson's prying eyes, though I wouldn't be surprised if she is on the lookout even at night for what she can see going on!

I went round to Clive's back door as I've been accustomed to doing lately. He always leaves the back door ajar if I say I might come over. I knocked gently, let myself in and closed the door. I didn't know why, but I felt immediately uneasy as I walked through Clive's kitchen and into the lounge. It was the freezer – it was a new one. The police have taken the chest one away for examination, and I don't imagine Clive fancies having it back anyway – that's if the police let him. There was something else: a perfume, and I knew I'd experienced that particular perfume before. Violets, that's what it was. Esther was wearing that perfume when I moved her body from the wheelchair to the freezer: *eau de violette*. The perfume seemed much stronger as I entered the lounge.

"Who's there? Who is it?" a woman's voice called. I'd heard a voice like that before, I was sure, but more strident and harsh than this one.

I froze suddenly as she came into view in the lounge. I almost fainted with shock. ESTHER! No – how could it be? She was dead and buried, wasn't she? But there stood a woman, for all the world the image of Esther. But she was standing upright, and Esther could not do that. Same face, same hair, same expression – everything! Same perfume: violets! I felt myself slipping into oblivion.

"There, there, Martha, drink this. You'll soon feel better. Come on, now – take a drink." It was Clive's voice, and it seemed to be coming from a long way off.

I must have fainted. I couldn't see properly at first – everything looked blurred – but slowly I began to feel strength returning to my body. My head began to clear and I was beginning to focus. Clive had his arm round my shoulders for support.

"I – I . ." I began.

"Don't try to talk just yet. We know what caused this, Martha. It's Rachel here – this is Esther's sister on a surprise visit, come to see me. This is Esther's identical-twin sister. She's the image of Esther, as you can see," Clive explained.

"Hello, my dear. It must have given you a turn. Clive had no idea I was coming – I thought I'd surprise him. I didn't realise you knew Esther, dear. I know she was never in the habit of seeing anyone but Clive – just one of her funny ways. Are you feeling a bit better now, my dear?" Rachel asked.

"Yes, thank you. It was just a shock," I told her.

"That's good. Yes, as Clive says, I'm Esther's twin sister. I've been living in Australia for many years and have only just managed to get to England this week. It's been a dreadful shock to me to realise what's happened to my dear sister – the poor darling, she didn't deserve to suffer such an end. I only hope and pray they catch the devil who did this and quickly!"

She turned away and I knew she was weeping quietly. I tried hard to pull myself together.

"I am so very sorry about what happened to your sister. Forgive me for making a fuss, but just seeing you like that in the half-light from the kitchen . . . Well, I knew it couldn't be Esther, of course, but . . ." I stammered.

"Yes, it would be a shock, Martha," Clive said. "It was a shock to me when I opened the door to Rachel. I had no idea she'd be able to come all this way, but it's good to see her."

"You don't even have my address in Australia, do you, Clive?"

"No, indeed, and I have no phone number for you. It was only that I came across an address of a neighbour you used to have down under, and I wrote enclosing an account of Esther's death in the hope that somehow the news might find you," Clive explained.

"It did find me eventually, but too late for me to get here for Esther's funeral."

"Anyway, you're here now. It's a pity we lost touch with one another. It must be sixteen years, Rachel, since we've had contact."

"More like eighteen," Rachel said. "And I didn't know you'd moved, Clive, and I didn't know how I'd find you. It was the police back in Oz who found your address for me through their enquiries. Of course it all took time and, as you see, I've arrived here eventually," Rachel explained.

"You can stay here as long as you wish, Rachel," Clive said.

"Thank you, Clive, but I won't be staying long. I'll make a visit to Esther's grave and then I must go back home. You remember my husband, George, had a bad car accident nearly twenty years ago. He's never recovered properly since and now he's got dementia. I've had to put him in respite so I could come here. I must get back to him as soon as possible."

"I do remember about the car accident," Clive said. "That's when we lost touch, and Esther and I moved house twice since then. I'm sorry about George. We all seem to be suffering one way and another just at present."

"Well, it's like this," Rachel said: "I can't do any good staying here. The damage is done. It's done and Esther's gone from us for ever! Oh, Clive!" And Rachel broke down, sobbing uncontrollably.

This time it was Rachel that Clive was comforting, not me. I felt very uneasy indeed. I wished I'd never gone over to Clive's.

"If there's anything I can do . . ." I said.

"No need, Martha – I'll look after Rachel. She'll be all right. We've a lot of catching up to do, though it doesn't seem as if she's able to stay here for long," Clive said.

"Well, if you're sure, Clive, but may I say how very sorry I am to meet you in such tragic circumstances, Rachel. I'll be going now as I'm sure you and Clive have much to talk about after all these years."

"Goodbye, my dear," Rachel said.

Clive took a few steps forward, saying, "Are you sure you're OK, Martha?"

"Yes, certain," I replied.

"I'll see you out, then."

I turned and gave a goodbye gesture to Rachel and left the house.

Outside the front door, Clive asked me if I was all right after the shock of seeing Rachel, especially as she so resembled Esther. I assured him I was fine, though secretly I was anything but! I could do without shocks like that! The scent of violets hung about me as I closed my front door.

***

I kept clear of Clive for the next couple of days. I'd really no wish to see Rachel again – she reminded me too vividly of Esther! The face haunted me in my dreams. In my quieter moments I reviewed the situation. Over six months now I've known Clive, six months now I've been attracted to him; five of these months I realised I was in love with him. Although we don't see much of each other (and we certainly don't go out on dates like normal couples), we are both well aware of the depth of our understanding and regard for each other. It is something that has deepened as time goes on. And yet the idea that one day we'll be together seems more distant than ever. There are so many complications. I've had several disappointments in my life, but I know in my heart that if ever Clive goes out of my life I'll never come to terms with it. There'll be a dreadful void.

Chapter 30

Jim! I'd nearly forgotten – he hasn't had his evening meal. Good Lord, is it quarter to eight? He's usually had his meal by seven and all cleared away. It's a wonder he hasn't been knocking on the floor for me. Perhaps he has! I'm sure he could get downstairs if he wanted to, but he never tries to do it, never has in the ten years we've lived here – well, not so far as I know, anyway. When he gets desperate over something he just knocks loudly on the floor with an old ebony walking stick that he's used since he came here. He has this notion that he's lame or something, and he believes he would be unable to make it downstairs even if he wanted to. So he's convinced himself he just has to stay upstairs – always! I'll go and make him a meal before he starts complaining.

For a change I made him pork rashers. He seemed to enjoy them. He was quite chatty too – kept saying how pleased he was with himself. About what exactly, though, he didn't say.

"Jim, isn't your speech good these days? I can understand everything you say," I told him.

"Of course it's clear. There was never anything wrong with it. It's you there's something wrong with, but I see you've got your proper voice back now," Jim said. Then he laughed loudly for a good minute.

I didn't bother to reason with him about his remarks – just one of his mad patches, I expect.

"Tell him – tell him to come and see me on Friday," Jim said.

"You mean Clive, over the road?" I asked. "I thought you'd forgotten all about that, Jim."

"Forget? It's you who forgets. That man, Clive, his wife has come back, you know. I saw her out of the window. She isn't dead and she told lies to everybody," Jim said.

"Told lies? How do you make that out, Jim?"

"Made out she was in a wheelchair – couldn't walk," said Jim.

"Yes, that's right, Jim."

No use explaining to him about Rachel, I thought. Evidently Jim was getting a bit better at remembering some things, but he got his facts mixed up.

"I'll see if Clive can come over on Friday, then, Jim."

"Yes, Friday – it's got to be Friday," Jim insisted.

***

I only had one letter this morning. Well, not a letter exactly – it was a birthday card. It's my forty-seventh birthday today. My sister sent me the card – she never forgets. There isn't anyone else who would remember. We've only a handful of distant relatives and I put a stop to any contact with them many years ago – on account of Jim, you see. Well, they think he's dead and buried, don't they?

Clive asked me, funnily enough, a couple of weeks ago, when my birthday was, but I avoided giving the exact date. I don't know why I did that really. As for Jim, he doesn't have a clue when my birthday is. I'm not sure he realises other people do have birthdays. Somehow he seems to think he's the only one who has one! What I usually do is buy myself something I've been wanting for a long time – something which I'd put off getting normally as I'd think I was being far too extravagant. This time, though, I haven't bought myself a thing. I don't seem able to bother about things like that at present, not with all that's been going on.

My sister put a short letter in with her card to me saying how very much she'd enjoyed her holiday abroad and telling me she'd met a 'gentleman' there who was writing to her! My! Don't say romance is running in the family! We're late developers, I suppose! I never see my sister in that light somehow. Still, it can happen to the most unlikely of us at times – take me, for example.

There's a strong smell of furniture polish coming from upstairs this morning. It's Jim. He's been putting a real shine on the coffins up there.

That's the second spray can of polish he's had from me in a week. Still, if it keeps him happy . . .

When I looked out of the window I saw Clive was cutting the grass in the front garden. That is to say he was trying to cut the grass, except that Mrs Jackson was talking ten to the dozen to him and he had to keep stopping to listen to her. It was fully ten minutes before she went in and left him to his work. Clive finished the mowing, and he was just putting the lawnmower away in his garage when a police car stopped at his gate. Two police officers got out, went up the drive and spoke to Clive. A minute later the three of them went indoors. I saw Mrs Jackson out again watching all this. She banged some milk bottles about on her front porch as if that was the purpose of her outing.

It worried me when I saw the police at Clive's house for I was well aware they never give up on a case – especially a case of murder! They must have stayed at Clive's at least half an hour. I did not see them come out, but I did see the back of a police car disappearing up the road. Now, I wonder what all that was about.

Chapter 31

Shortly afterwards I was to find out, and who else would be so prompt with the gossip? You're right: Mrs Jackson was over here in a flash!

"Yes, dear, he just told me those men – you know, the ones suspected of the robberies round here – well, they've released one of them, but they've kept the other two because they did do a break-in evidently on Grosvenor Road. They stole a camera and some money! But as for Clive's house and the strangling and all that, well, they say it wasn't them and they've let them go. Makes you think, doesn't it, dear?"

Mrs Jackson it was indeed with her latest 'newsflash'.

"But I thought they'd only got two suspects the other week?"

"I know that's what it said in the paper, didn't it, dear? But there must have been three for questioning. Clive's just been telling me. Poor man, he looks more worried now than ever. That woman's gone, you know – that sister-in-law of his. Mind you, I didn't get to talk to her. Seems she lives in Australia. Clive wasn't very forthcoming when I asked about her. Mind you, it might very well not have been his sister-in-law. He could just have said she was, couldn't he? For all we know she might have been some fancy woman he'd had staying there," Mrs Jackson said.

"Really, that's a dreadful thing to say about Clive. He's such a nice man. No, I'm sure you're wrong there, Mrs Jackson," I said.

I know there can be no substance to her unkind remarks, but I still find myself feeling a little jealous at the mere suggestion of such a thing.

This feeling of jealousy is new to me – I can't recall ever feeling this way about anyone or anything before. It is a pointer to the depth of my regard for Clive, no doubt.

"Well, you can think what you like, dear, but it wouldn't surprise me in the least. Not that it's any of my business what he does. He's a free agent now, isn't he? You want to watch it, dear – he might be after you next! It's been my experience that they're always at their most vulnerable following a bereavement. I've seen it too often to be wrong."

I gave a half-smile as she aired her observations, and I tried to appear as normal as possible. I hoped I hadn't given anything away, although I felt quite angry and defensive of Clive after what she had implied.

"Well, dear, they'll just have to start looking again, won't they?" Mrs Jackson said.

"Who will?" I asked.

"Why, the police, of course. Really, dear, you never seem to have your mind on what I'm telling you these days. I said the other week, dear, it's all getting too much for you with that man of yours upstairs. Stands to reason all this time it must be affecting you. And then there's your age, of course. You know what I mean, dear. Oh, I had a dreadful time myself when I came to the change – hot flushes, headaches, depression, the lot! I suffered, I can tell you. Well, I must go – can't stop talking here all day. See you later, dear, and do take care, won't you?"

And once again she was gone. What a woman! I should think she'd be enough to drive a man of even the soundest mind insane!

Chapter 32

It was late that afternoon when I went over to see Clive. His sister-in-law had left, he told me. She had said she would call in at the police station to say who she was and see if she could shed any light on what had happened to her sister, though she was sure she wouldn't be able to. Also she thought she might possibly learn a bit more about how the case was progressing, though she didn't hold out much hope of that either. She went to the cemetery after that to see where Esther was buried. She told Clive she was also going to London to look up an old school friend of hers prior to her flight home to Australia. Clive offered to go to the cemetery with her, but she insisted she would rather go alone and Clive respected her wishes.

"I wonder how Rachel got on with the police, Clive? I can't see she could have been any help to them or they to her, but they'd hardly have failed to notice how like Esther she looks when they have their files out with pictures of Esther in front of them," I remarked.

"That's true," Clive agreed. "It was no wonder you passed out the other evening here on seeing Rachel. She and Esther are so alike, not just in looks either – in mannerisms, everything. I could hardly bring myself to look her full in the face when she was here. If I did it was Esther I saw all the time and I feared I'd betray myself in some way. I kept seeing myself with my hands clenched tight round Esther's neck. Oh, God, Martha, it was awful! I think through all of this if it hadn't been for you, my dear, I'd have gone out of my mind! Will I never be free of the nightmare of what I did?"

I went over to him, putting my arms round him and holding him close as a mother might cradle her child.

"Clive, please don't – please don't torture yourself with those dreadful thoughts. What's done is done."

"And cannot be undone," Clive said.

"Yes, I've heard those words somewhere before too, but this is no play-acting, Clive."

We sat together, me stroking and smoothing his ruffled hair in a soothing gesture. After a few seconds he seemed more himself again.

"You'd have thought, wouldn't you, Martha, that Rachel might have stayed a little longer – especially after travelling halfway round the world to get here? Evidently she didn't wish to. On the other hand, I can't say I ever knew her very well."

"How long did you know Rachel for?" I asked.

"I only knew her briefly for a few weeks before I married Esther. Soon after that Rachel moved to Australia and I didn't see her again until she arrived here the other day."

"Did she ever write?" I asked.

"She did at first, but then it seemed to die a natural death," Clive remarked, and an involuntary shiver went right through me.

Clive was quick to notice this too.

"Sorry, Martha – it was just a figure of speech. Oh, Martha, how I wish we could both disappear now, away from everything, away from this wretched place," Clive said.

"I wish that too, Clive. You know I do, but it cannot be. Whatever happens we must make it appear that things are as normal as possible – until, that is, the police bring things to a satisfactory end, which I pray will happen soon."

"Which they will not do. How can they? No, the case will only be at an end when they discover who murdered Esther!"

"Don't let's talk about it, Clive. Constant worrying won't make things any better, although I know that's easy to say. It will be best if I carry on like I'm the occasional helpful neighbour, and then who's to suspect anything? We've got to be brave, Clive – we've got to hold on and, in a little while, who knows? Our wildest dreams may come true," I said.

"Oh, Martha, you are indeed my own dearest Martha. Please let it be so – oh, please, God, let it be so!"

We embraced for a long moment before he could say more, and this seemed to calm him and close the conversation – for the time being, at least.

"Oh, Clive, I nearly forgot the real reason I'm here. It's about Jim. He hasn't forgotten about wanting to see you. He wants to know if you'll come on Friday – he insists it's a Friday. Don't ask me why, but there it is. Can you do that?"

"Of course," Clive said. "What time?"

"In the evening, I think, would be best, after he's had his meal – say about seven o'clock? Well, between seven and half past," I suggested.

"Fine, Martha. I'll be there. I'm quite looking forward to seeing this Jim of yours!"

"You may change your mind on that one after you've met him. There's no knowing what he might say to you, Clive. He gets things so mixed up in his mind. He could say anything, so don't be surprised."

"Can I bring him anything? A couple of beers?" Clive enquired.

"No, no. Anyway, he's not supposed to have alcohol with the medication he's on."

"Oh, I didn't think of that. I'll look forward to Friday, then."

"I must go now, Clive."

"Wait a moment, Martha. I have something for you. I won't be a minute."

As I waited I sniffed the air and there it was again – the scent of violets. That perfume, only this time the smell was less intense. I don't see myself fancying violets ever again!

"Sorry to be so long. I mislaid it. Here you are, Martha – it's for you. Open it," Clive said.

Clive handed me a small box-shaped package with pretty silver-and-blue wrapping paper.

"For me? What is it?" I asked.

"Open it and see," said Clive.

I sat down again and Clive joined me, eagerly watching me open the package. I removed the wrapping paper to reveal a small white-and-gold box. Inside there was a ring – an eternity ring, a sparkling circlet of small stones set in platinum. They were diamonds!

"For me, Clive? For me?" I said excitedly.

"Who else? Put it on, Martha."

The ring slipped comfortably on my wedding-ring finger. How beautiful, and yet how delicate it looked as I held up my hand to see the full effect! I've never been given anything so expensive in my life before. I was quite overcome.

"Oh, Clive, it is so beautiful. I don't know what to say. What have I done to deserve this?"

"My dear Martha, I want, by some small token, to put a seal on our relationship. Please keep it and wear it for me. It will be a symbol to bind us in our love and understanding of one another," Clive said.

"Oh, Clive, I'll wear it always. Thank you. It is so beautiful. It must have cost a fortune. You shouldn't have spent so much on me."

"It's nothing compared to your worth to me, Martha!"

Before I could say more, we kissed tenderly several times.

"I'll wear this ring and treasure it, Clive, always – I promise. What a wonderful surprise you've given me!"

"I am only too pleased you like it, Martha, and that it fits so well."

"Thank you, my dearest. Now, hard as it is to leave you, I must get back to Jim and tell him you'll see him on Friday."

I kissed Clive again and went quickly to my house. I looked at my beautiful ring and felt about eighteen!

Chapter 33

Jim's meal was prepared in double-quick time on Friday evening. I took it to him and, much to my surprise, he ate every bit of it. He even asked for an extra helping of chocolate ice cream, which surprised me. He seemed in good form for a change.

"Is he coming or is he not?" Jim asked.

"If you mean Clive, yes, he is. He said he'd be over between seven and half past. Oh, there's the doorbell now. That'll be him."

"Yes, hurry up, will you? I've been waiting a long time for this." And Jim gave one of his loud laughs.

"This way, Clive – Jim's upstairs. He's really looking forward to meeting you," I said. I spoke in a particularly loud voice for I wanted Jim to hear all I said.

I walked into Jim's room ahead of Clive.

"Here he is, Jim – here's Clive. Say hello."

Clive stood uneasily in the doorway. I could tell he was somewhat taken aback by Jim's appearance. Jim, you see, had dressed himself up for the visit, which was all well and good except that he looked like he was in mourning. He had his black suit on, black shoes and a black tie. He was even wearing black gloves! I'd decided not to remark on it myself when I saw him dressed so earlier on. It could have been, after all, just Jim's way of showing respect to his visitor – it was such a rare occurrence to have one!

"Come in, come in. Sit down – no, not there; over there in the corner, where you used to sit, opposite me."

Clive did as instructed and sat opposite Jim.

"That's better," Jim said.

Clive proffered his hand for a hand-shake, but Jim waved him on to be seated.

"No, don't move – stay still there, Clive. You haven't changed one little bit. Oh yes, it's just like old times – you over there in the corner. Don't you think so, eh?" Jim asked.

"Er, yes, I suppose it is," Clive said.

I'd warned Clive earlier that it was always best to go along with whatever Jim was talking about. After all, he thought he knew what he meant even if nobody else did! I sat on a chair near the door. How strange it seemed to see the two of them together – the two men in my life you might say, but for very different reasons!

"You know, Clive, I was very upset when you went away and left me," Jim said.

"I'm sorry if I upset you. May I call you Jim?"

"Well, you always did before, for God's sake!"

"Yes, I did, Jim, didn't I? Well, I'm very glad to see you again after all this time," Clive said.

For someone usually shy and awkward, I must say I thought Clive was managing the situation remarkably well.

"I was beginning to think you'd never come back, Clive, but you're here now and that's all that matters to me," Jim said. Jim then turned his attention to me: "Oh, you're still here, are you, Martha? Go away – go on, leave us. This is my friend, not yours. Go on – away, I say!" Jim shouted loudly.

I sat downstairs with the door open wide so I could catch what went on upstairs. I must say Clive looked surprised at Jim's outburst, but he didn't interfere. I picked up the paper for something to do, but I wasn't really reading. I couldn't catch all that was being said upstairs, but I did hear most of it.

"Well, you see, Clive, it's her – Martha. I have to stay here to look after her. Oh yes, she's gone off her head, you know. Most days she's fairly normal, but some days . . . Well, she acts so strange that I wonder how much longer I can stand it," Jim told Clive.

"What way is she strange, Jim?" Clive asked.

"Every way. Well, every way when it's one of her bad days. She left her husband – David's his name – and on account of this she takes it out on me!" Jim said.

"Does she, now? And where's this David now?"

"I don't know, but she left him a few times. Here – listen to this: she was even trying to get me to marry her at one time!"

"What did you say to that, Jim?"

"What did I say? Well, I made it quite clear I wasn't having any, didn't I? No fear – not with her in her state of mind. That's why I have to look after her, you see," Jim said.

"Oh yes, I understand that, Jim."

"And what's more, Clive, she won't let anybody in to see me. She got rid of my friends years ago."

"Don't you ever go out, Jim?"

"Go out? Never. She won't let me. She tried to poison me, you know, once, and I nearly died. Well, I'm still affected by it. It's my legs, you see. It left me partly paralysed and I can't get down the stairs now. Oh, I tell you, Clive, she's a wicked woman! I'm very surprised she's let you in here again," Jim said.

"What do you mean *again*, Jim?"

"Don't start confusing me, Clive. You know damned well you used to be here regularly sitting where you are now. She's put you up to this, hasn't she? The bitch! Don't trust her, Clive. She's no good to you or me. She's no good to anybody." And Jim gave vent to his raucous laugh once more.

As I said before, I heard most of their conversation, but even I was taken aback at what Jim had just said. I'd no idea that Jim thinks me such a bad lot. He was very confused in his thinking today – worse than he'd been for some time. Strange how Jim thinks of me sometimes as Martha and at other times I am Maggie. Poor Clive! I wondered what he made of it all. I thought it was time for some refreshments.

"Here we are, gentlemen," I said. "Help yourselves."

I'd taken in a tray of assorted sandwiches and a large jug of coffee.

"Maggie, don't just leave it there; pour it out for us," Jim said.

"Oh, all right, Jim. I thought you didn't want my company – that's what you said before."

Clive just looked at me without speaking. He'd tell me later what he made of Jim, I knew. I also noticed that Jim had gone back to calling me Maggie.

'Leave him be,' I thought. 'He's in a grumpy enough mood as it is – with me, anyway, though he does appear to be liking Clive's company.'

"Maggie, open my private cupboard over there. Here's the key. Unlock it – go on," Jim said.

I duly obliged. It was the first time I'd ever been allowed to open Jim's cupboard. He always kept it securely locked.

"Have you found it, then?" Jim asked.

"I might, Jim, if you tell me what I am supposed to be looking for," I replied.

"The flask, woman! Give it here," Jim shouted.

I felt about. The drawer inside was quite deep and full of oddities, but eventually I found a hip flask.

"Is this what you want, Jim?"

"Of course it is. Give it here."

I passed it over to Jim. He unscrewed the top and took an almighty swig of whatever it was that was in it. Then he offered it to Clive.

"Go on, Clive – have a drop of this. It will do you a power of good," Jim said.

"What is it Jim? Whisky?" Clive asked.

"Never you mind what it is. Drink it – go on! It hasn't seen the light of day for ten years, but you're special, Clive!"

Clive raised the flask to his lips and took a small dose of whatever it was. By the look on his face he was not too enamoured of it. He handed the flask back to Jim.

"Hm, nice, Jim – very nice," Clive said.

"Nice? Nice? What do you mean *nice*? It isn't meant to be nice – it's meant to be powerful, man. It's meant to be powerful!" Jim said.

"Oh, it's that all right," Clive told him. "Yes, it's that sure enough. My head feels as if it doesn't belong to me. I feel like I'm floating somewhere, Jim."

Clive looked a little apprehensive.

"Floating, are you? I made it myself you know, a long time ago. Nobody but me knows how it's done either, do they, Maggie?"

"I wouldn't know about that, Jim. I never knew you'd made that stuff all those years ago. You never let on, did you?"

"There's a lot you don't know about me, Maggie. It wouldn't do to let you in on all my secrets, would it?" And Jim chortled to himself quietly as he thought about what he'd just said.

I have an uneasy feeling about Jim and his secret goings-on, whatever they might be. Perhaps he isn't always as daft as I think.

"Here – lock my cupboard and give me the key, Maggie. I can't trust you and you know it," Jim said.

I did Jim's bidding. I could see Clive wasn't exactly enjoying his visit to Jim. He looked even more troubled when Jim insisted he had another swig from the hip flask, but he complied as it seemed to keep Jim happy.

After a few minutes Clive got up to go.

"Sorry, Jim, but I'll have to leave you now. I don't feel too good. Sorry."

"Ah well, I suppose your wife will wonder where you are," Jim said.

"My wife?"

"Oh, it's all right, Clive – I know what's been going on. I know you've had troubles, like me. I know how wicked your wife was, pretending she couldn't walk and then, all of a sudden, I saw her from the window, bold as brass, walking up your path! But that's women for you, Clive. I tell you they're no good. You can't trust them. Believe me, I know. It's just as well I'm not married to Maggie here or goodness knows what would have happened. No, I may be handicapped, but I'm a free man as regards marriage matters and that's how I intend to stay, eh, Maggie?" Jim said.

"That's right, Jim – you stay as you are," I said. "But look – Clive has to go now, so say goodbye to him, Jim."

"Go if you must, Clive, but come again soon."

"Yes, I will, Jim. Goodnight."

Jim didn't answer. He just kept muttering to himself and staring at the ceiling.

I saw Clive out of the house and said we'd have a chat later on about his visit to Jim, when Jim couldn't hear any of the conversation. After all, the way Jim was at the moment there was no way of knowing what he would construe from anything he overheard.

"See you later, Clive," I whispered.

***

I've taken to going over to Clive's most evenings now. Usually we have a couple of drinks. It is uncanny the way we get on so very well with one another. It isn't what we say or do; it is just that there is a very happy atmosphere surrounding us whenever we are together. It is something I am willing to settle for any time rather than those mad, passionate affairs you can read about in women's magazines sometimes. Not that I've ever experienced one of those either, but I'm sure I wouldn't go much on one. They seldom seem to last, anyway, do they? What Clive and I have I know will last forever if we ever get the chance to see it through!

∗∗

About an hour after Clive had gone I heard the strangest sounds coming from upstairs: a kind of wild, out-of-tune singing. It was from Jim all right. I took one look at him when I went upstairs and I knew what was the matter with him at once.

"You're drunk, aren't you, Jim? Here – give that flask to me!" I said angrily.

I snatched it from him, which almost caused him to fall out of his chair as he tried to hang on to his flask.

"Here – give it back. You're a thief, a berloody thief!" Jim shouted in a slurred tone of voice.

I could see Jim was unsteady in his seat, so I went towards him and bodily lifted him back to a safer position.

"Don't touch me! Get away, you bitch! You won't beat me, never!"

"No, I don't suppose I ever will, Jim. Now, just settle down or Clive will never come to see you again, do you hear me?"

This seemed to quieten him somewhat. As he looked at me there were tears in his eyes.

He said, "You won't stop him coming, will you, Maggie?" And he began to sob like a child.

I couldn't help feeling a bit sorry for him when he reacted so. As I left him I noticed the fingers on his left hand were twitching convulsively. Downstairs I put Jim's flask on the draining board. I took the top off and took a sniff. The smell was peculiar – not like anything I'd come across before. There wasn't much left in the flask. I put the top back on. Whatever it was, it had inebriated Jim quite quickly. Then another thought struck me. Clive had drunk some of the stuff, hadn't he?

I wonder what effect it's had on him. But I know that Jim drank a lot more than Clive did.

I didn't go over to Clive's after the flask episode. I felt quite drained and hardly remember putting my head on the pillow. I slept soundly until next morning.

Chapter 34

I was awakened by a furious hammering on the front door. I wondered in my semi-conscious state who it could be. I elbowed clumsily into my dressing gown and made my way unsteadily downstairs. The banging continued.

"All right, all right, I'm coming."

I objected to my rude awakening. I unlocked the door and removed the chain catch.

"Oh, my God, Martha, let me in, let me in. Oh my, I don't know what to do!"

It was Mrs Jackson. What a state she was in, to be sure. I helped her into the lounge. She sat down on the settee. I wasn't sure she intended to do so – she seemed to fall on to the nearest support.

"There, there – calm yourself. Nothing can be that bad, can it? Whatever is wrong?" I asked.

"Well, it's like this, you see. I've been away. I went to stay with my sister. You know how unsettled I've been since I had that intruder in my place?"

"Yes, and you told me you might go to your sister's for a while."

"That's right. Oh, I went to my sister's all right, but on the second night what do you think? In the middle of the night – oh, God, Martha, it was just too horrendous. . . ." and Mrs Jackson fell to weeping.

I got her a drink.

"Here – drink this," I said.

Her hands were shaking as she took the glass.

"Where was I?" she asked me.

"You were saying about the middle of the night at your sister's" I told her.

"Was I? Oh yes. Well, I woke up and there he was – a big man! I couldn't see his face in the dark, but I could just make out his outline as he stood near the window. He came towards me. I was petrified!"

"Did he – did he . . ."

"Oh no, he didn't touch me. It was anything of value he was after. He grabbed my watch and my two diamond rings and my gold necklace from the bedside table. Then he put his big hand over my mouth – not that I could get out a squeak, never mind a scream – and then I must have passed out. My sister found me. I'd tumbled on to the floor and the noise had wakened her. The man was away, of course, by that time, and so was my jewellery!"

"How awful! You poor dear, it must indeed have been absolutely terrifying. Did you ring the police?"

"My sister did. They came round quite quickly, which was surprising seeing as it was the middle of the night! They said they were on the lookout for someone doing break-ins in the middle of the night as there'd been three in that area recently. They took fingerprints there and then, and statements. They didn't offer much hope of getting the stolen goods back, but promised to do their best."

"Oh, I don't know – I think the police are very good at catching people eventually."

I wished I hadn't said that when I considered my own situation and Clive's. We aren't exactly innocents, are we?

"Well, if it takes forever to find out who murdered Clive's wife, as it seems to be doing, we may never find out who broke into my sister's house!"

And that brings it all back to life again for Clive and for me. And that's how it's going to be: we'll never be free of the crime that Clive committed, and that I aided and abetted!

"Martha, Martha, did you hear what I just said to you?" Mrs Jackson asked. "Are you sure you're all right, dear? You were staring just now as if your mind was far away."

"Was I? Sorry – I was thinking what a dreadful experience you've had. Is there anything I can do to help?"

"I don't think there is, dear. It's made me feel a bit better just telling you about it," she said.

"I suppose you're glad to be home, then?"

"I'm not so sure of that. One place is nearly as bad as the other as things have turned out. I mean, I had an intruder in my house here and then at my sister's. My nerves won't stand much more, they really won't!"

"You should see your doctor, Mrs Jackson. I'm sure he'll be able to give you something that will help," I told her.

"Yes, you're right – I could do with something. And speaking of doctors, you should see yours too, dear. You've been getting far too absent-minded lately. Your mind doesn't seem to be on what you're doing. Go before it's too late," she warned me.

"I'll think about it."

And before I could say anything further she was up and out, dashing across the road to her house. Well, I suppose I come in useful at times, even if it's only listening to someone else's troubles.

And that reminds me of my other trouble: Jim. How is he this morning? I'll go and find out.

"Fast asleep still!" I said to myself. I've hardly ever known Jim to sleep so late in all the years we've lived here."

"Good Lord! Would you believe it?" I gasped aloud, for there, clasped in his hand, was the flask! The one I'd put in the kitchen on the draining board the night before. However could it have moved upstairs?

'There's more to Jim than meets the eye,' I thought!

I tried at first to remove the flask from Jim's clenched hand, but I decided to leave it as I didn't wish to wake him yet. After the state he was in last night it was probably best to let him sleep for as long as he could. I went back downstairs and into the kitchen. No, I wasn't mistaken: there was Jim's flask on the draining board where I had left it the previous evening. How could that be? Well, Jim must have two flasks, not one.He had a second flask in his hand upstairs! He may have taken swigs from that one and really knocked himself out for the night! Hence the long sleep!

It was almost lunchtime when Jim came to. I took him some tea and toast. He was looking a bit worse for wear.

And talking of wearing, I said, "Jim, why did you go to bed in your suit?"

"Go to bed in my suit? What do you take me for, Martha – an idiot? I've just got up and dressed, haven't I? Sometimes I wonder what is to become of you," Jim said, and he fixed his eyes on the floor, his hands forcibly held on his knees, as if it was taking a great effort to keep himself steady.

I said no more and went downstairs.

As I did so, Jim shouted after me, "And I don't want disturbing today, do you hear? I've some little jobs to do on my woodwork, so remember!"

Chapter 35

I decided to get my hair done that afternoon. I'd rung up and made an appointment. I said I wasn't sure what I wanted done exactly. I'd take advice on that one. Very seldom did I visit a hairdresser. I'd caught sight of myself in the hall mirror and what a drab, frumpy old image met my gaze! Yes, time to improve matters, I determined, even if it was only by a visit to the hairdresser! It wouldn't do wonders, I knew, but it would no doubt do something.

Now, take Mrs Jackson (and there are times when I wish somebody would!). Charity! Charity! Martha, what would your father have said if he'd heard you? Funny how my father has been in my thoughts more than once lately. He was a stern but loving man to his family. Nothing could ever make him change his mind once it was made up. He was the original man of principles. He pronounced them and he certainly lived by them, and he did his level best to see his family observed them as well. I can't remember ever answering my father back or going against him in any major issues – especially moral ones. Oh, he was a great man for moral standards was my father. He'd have a fit if he came back to today's world and saw what goes on! It's just as well he can't – he'd never be able to cope, much less understand it. He wouldn't be too pleased with me either, the way my life has evolved!

But enough of that – back to hairdressing and Mrs Jackson, who spends a fortune on her hair every week. It's either a perm or a new cut or a shampoo and set or a blow-dry. Last week she told me she's found a new up-to-the-minute salon opened, and she's made an appointment to have a head massage and her legs waxed! Still, she must be able to afford it. I do know for a fact that she's pretty well off. You've only to see her furniture and carpets – beautiful Chinese carpets and rugs. I did see one like she has in her hallway in a posh high-street furniture shop last week. It was marked up for over £1,000! I doubt if all the carpet in this house cost that much! Still, good luck to her. As they say, you only live once.

So it was going to be my turn today to 'live it up' by having a hairdo. Modest by Chinese-rug standards, I know, but it would suit me just fine.

'I know,' I thought: 'it'll be the birthday present to myself that I never bought.' That's what comes of being brought up to be careful with money. I always feel I have to justify to myself for any small extravagance. I got a large bequest in a will years ago, but I'm careful how I dip into it. I've always got Jim's needs and his doctors to consider!

It looked like I'd be out for most of the day. There was the shopping and the hairdo and I'd have to see how Clive was. Jim wouldn't worry – didn't he say he didn't want disturbing as he'd adjustments to make to his woodwork? Well, let him get on with it. He'd been so grumpy I was glad to get out. I can't seem to say anything that pleases him these days. He was even a bit short with Clive, considering Clive is the first person, apart from me, he's spoken to in ten long years. I still can't come to terms with the idea that Jim thinks Clive has visited him several times in the past; that he has in fact sat opposite Jim on many occasions. I remember Jim used to stare into the corner opposite to him often enough and carry on imaginary conversations with 'somebody'. I don't expect I'll ever know the explanation for that one.

I washed up the few dirty dishes, tidied the kitchen and got ready to go out. Oh, look – there's the flask from last night, Jim's flask, the one I took from him last night after his drinking session with Clive. That's it, then: Jim does have another flask just like this one and he's got it with him!

Just before I went out of the front door I remembered I really should have rung the rodent officer at the City Cleansing Department. Oh, I'll do it later – maybe tomorrow. I didn't want to be late for my hair appointment. We've had an invasion of mice, you see. Nearly every house on our side of the street has evidence of mouse activity, such as bits of waste food or newspapers gnawed and such, and I found several patches of mouse droppings in the shed. The old chap next door swears he's seen at least two rats in his garden, and Mrs Brown's dog – next door but one – actually caught a rat and killed it! Somebody said they'd all appeared in our area since the demolition of the old flour mill started not 100 yards away. It was at the back of our properties. I didn't like the idea of rodents anywhere near me. I even bought some rat poison myself and sprinkled it in the most likely places, but I don't know if it's done any good yet. You've to be careful with that stuff if you have any pets. Some of my neighbours have dogs and they wouldn't thank anybody for keeping vermin down at the expense of harming their pets, I know.

I shouted "Bye" to Jim, but he didn't answer. That is nothing unusual, mind you. Sometimes he does answer, and sometimes he doesn't. It just depends on the mood he is in.

Chapter 36

"Hello there, dear. Getting on the bus, are we?"

It was Mrs Jackson.

"Yes, just going to town," I said.

"That's nice – we can sit on the bus together."

There were only a couple of other passengers on the bus when it arrived. We boarded and sat at the front. My, but she was dressed up today – beautiful fur coat, sort of grey squirrel. I hadn't seen her in that one before. Her shoes were real leather, and her handbag. She must have noticed me staring at her coat.

"Do you like it, dear? It's supposed to be real mink."

"Yes, it's beautiful, and it does suit you," I said.

"Yes, I like it myself. I've only just bought it. To be honest, I bought it from my sister. She's never worn it, you know. It was the last present her husband bought her before he died – a week before he passed on, to be precise – and of course she couldn't take to it after that. No, it's never been worn. So when I said I liked it she said I could have it. Well, naturally I felt I couldn't just take it like that, could I? No, I insisted on paying at least half the value, and after a big argument she gave in. So here I am – the proud new owner!"

"You got a bargain, I'm sure," I told her.

"I should just think I did, dear, for £400! It'll do nicely for the winter. Tell me: have you spoken to Clive recently?"

"As a matter of fact, he was over at my house yesterday."

"No! Clive in your house? My, my! Does Jim know?"

"It was at Jim's request that Clive was there," I said.

Mrs Jackson looked quite amazed, to say the least!

"You mean after all these years Jim wanted to see somebody other than you?"

"That's right."

"Well, that does surprise me. All these years never going out, dear, and refusing to see anyone but you, and then he asks to see a complete stranger! Words fail me, they really do."

She was actually silent for at least two minutes. Then she burst out suddenly as if she could contain herself no longer: "But why Clive, dear? Why him?"

"Don't ask me because I can't tell you. All I know is that Jim was quite insistent that Clive should visit him, and so I arranged it. I did warn Clive that anything might happen, but it didn't go off too badly. Clive sat with Jim for quite a time. The strange thing was that Jim kept saying Clive had been with him many times before, which I know has never happened. I think Jim enjoyed Clive's visit in his own peculiar way."

"And will Clive be seeing Jim again?"

"Maybe. Jim seemed quite anxious that he should," I told her.

"The reason I asked if you'd seen Clive, dear, is that I caught sight of him this morning when I got back home and I thought he looked quite poorly. I asked him if he was all right and he just nodded and went indoors. There was something not right there, though, you mark my words. He may follow in his wife's footsteps, so to speak, if he doesn't look after himself!"

"Oh, don't say that, Mrs Jackson. It's probably just a passing upset," I told her.

"I hope you're right, dear, but he looked very dodgy to me. Oh, here's our stop. You going to the shops, dear?"

"Yes, I am."

We both left our seats and got off the bus.

We walked along the High Street for half its length, then Mrs Jackson said, "Well, dear, I'll say goodbye here. I've got some business to attend to at the offices over the road. I may catch up with you on the bus back, eh?"

"Yes, maybe," I replied.

I carried on down the road.

What did she say? Clive looked dreadful – might be following in his wife's footsteps? A shiver went through me as I thought about it. I knew now I should have checked on Clive before coming to town. Too late now, but I decided I would certainly do that later.

It was then I realised I'd gone right past one of the very shops I wanted to go into.

I must keep my mind on what I'm doing. Perhaps Mrs Jackson is right: she's remarked more than once about my appearing absent-minded and not taking in what she's said. And there's Jim too trying to make out I'm not all there. It just seems to me that everything I do these days is overshadowed by thoughts of Clive and all that's happened.

"Oh, I do beg your pardon," I said as I had evidently walked straight into someone.

"That's all right, my dear. No harm done – just an accident," a rather hoarse voice said.

When I looked more closely I saw it was an old lady I had bumped into – a very slight old lady – well over eighty, I should imagine – and she carried a white stick. That made me feel even more guilty.

"Oh dear, I really am so sorry. Are you sure you're all right?" I asked anxiously.

"Yes, dear – don't worry. I quite often have little collisions when I'm out. I expect it was as much my fault as yours," she said.

"Not at all – the fault was all mine. I should look where I am going, shouldn't I?"

"I'm just fine," the old lady insisted.

"Well, if you're sure," I said, and I wished her "Good day."

"Goodbye, dear."

And the old lady went off at a good deal faster rate than I had thought her capable of!

I did what I had to do round the shops, and then I went off in search of my hair appointment. I felt quite excited at the prospect of 'a new look'. This was something of a treat for me. It was quite an expensive salon. I'd never been there before.

"Would madam come this way, please," a tall, beautiful girl asked.

"Oh, me? Yes, certainly," I said and I followed her. I'd never been called a madam before.

We went through beaded curtains which jangled like the rolling of dice as we passed through. The light seemed brighter on the other side and there were pleasant smells all around.

"If madam would take a seat for a few moments our style advisor will be with you shortly."

"Oh, thank you," I said as the girl motioned me to a chair.

There were four chairs in a row, all upholstered in a rich deep-pink velvet, buttoned tightly, pulling the velvet into diamond shapes. Expensive magazines lay at random, displaying all the stuff that ordinary people can only dream of buying. Still, it's nice to look.

The first two chairs were occupied by two middle-aged most elegantly dressed women. They weren't beautiful, but they'd certainly made the very best of themselves one way and another. They obviously knew one another very well and were having an involved conversation.

"And do you know, Felicity, they'd only been married a year when he went off with that other woman!" said the silver-haired lady sitting next to me.

"Practically since the minute he married Vanessa. I mean, it was obvious from the start to anyone with eyes to see: he only married her for her money," said the first speaker.

"I believe that's true. It's just such a pity that the only person who didn't realise that was Vanessa, the poor darling. I feel for her, I really do," said the blue rinse.

They would have carried on, I've no doubt, had not two more of the elegant salon girls come forward. One called for the first madam to follow her for her beauty-mask treatment and the other called the second madam to follow her to the massage parlour.

It was my turn next. A tall, slender blonde asked me to follow her to the styling advisory area, which I did.

It certainly is upmarket here, I'll give them that. Mind you, the prices are upmarket too, which I suppose is to be expected.

Well, I felt like being extravagant today. I didn't care for once. Jim and his caskets seemed rather remote at that moment. After several minutes' discussion and viewing various styles, the advisor came up with something I liked. She said it would give me a more youthful appearance! Well, I am all for that.

Next I was passed on to Deirdre, who evidently was totally to transform my appearance. Where did all these beautiful girls come from? Every one of them must have been hand-picked for the job. Deirdre wasted no time in setting about me with a will. I began to feel quite helpless as locks of hair were lopped off, falling on to the floor on all sides of me. I felt a bit nervous and I began to wonder if she'd leave me any hair on! A light perm was next, although I hadn't intended that when I booked in.

"It's the only way, madam," Deirdre informed me. "Madam needs 'body' in her hair after the cut, and this perm will provide that," she told me.

Just over two hours later I was transformed. I was shown the result from all angles, and I must say that once I overcame the initial shock of the shortness of my hair I quite like it. Yes, and I believe it does make me look a bit younger.

"I hope madam likes the new style – so easy to manage too," Deirdre said.

"Yes, I think it looks very nice, thank you."

"And if madam would like to pay at the cash desk over there . . ." And Deirdre was gone, presumably to face her next challenge.

I must say I was a bit shocked at the cost of the hairdo: £16 was not exactly what I had in mind, posh salon or no posh salon! But I got on with it and paid up. There was a fancy box on the counter for leaving tips for the girls, and I felt obliged to contribute: another £3!

'I might as well play the part,' I thought.

And let's face it, Mrs Jackson goes there nearly every week, doesn't she? Need I say more?

As I left the salon I was just in time to see the two well-to-do ladies I'd been sitting next to in the waiting area. They were being chauffeur-driven away at speed down the High Street.

'The idle rich!' I thought. 'I think I could get used to that kind of life myself, if I ever get the chance!'

I must say the hair do has done something for me. I stepped out with a much more positive attitude. I held my head high and felt almost important for once. I bought a few essentials I'd forgotten and a half-bottle of brandy for Clive. It might help him if he isn't feeling too good. I decided to call in and see him on the way home.

I permitted myself one more extravagance before I went for the bus: I went to the florist's shop and bought myself a dozen red roses. Silly really, I suppose, but I've always dreamed of someone sending me a dozen red roses and it has never happened, so I bought them for myself on impulse. I did an even dafter thing after that: I asked to have them delivered to my address and actually wrote out a card to myself. It read, 'To Martha with love.' I got the florist to write that on the card. I must be mad. Yes, that's what Jim called me. I'd better watch it!

I went straight to the bus stop from there. Luckily a bus came along almost at once. I got on it and sat at the back. It was nearly empty except for an old couple. I was glad Mrs Jackson wasn't on it. I didn't feel like talking to her or anybody else right then.

It is only a twenty-minute journey from town to where I live, but I nearly missed my stop. I actually felt myself dozing off when I closed my eyes for a few moments. Some inner sense jerked me back to consciousness as the bus slowed to a halt – my stop. It was fortunate the old couple were getting off at my stop. It gave me time to catch up with them.

A minute later I was level with Clive's gate. I went up the drive and rang the front doorbell. It was some seconds before I got an answer. I heard an unlocking going on, and then the door opened a fraction. There was Clive in his dressing gown and slippers looking very much under the weather. He let me in. I put my parcels down in the hallway.

"Don't stand there, Clive. Get in the lounge where it's warmer. You look dreadful."

We went into the lounge and sat down.

"And you look wonderful, Martha. Your hair – I like it," Clive told me.

"Thanks, Clive. Yes, I went mad today and had it done. Let me turn the gas fire up; you look so cold."

I did the honours and we both immediately felt the benefit.

"There – that's better. Tell me honestly, Clive: how are you?"

"To be honest, not good at all. I can't think what's gone wrong with me. I'm never ill, you know. Well, at least I haven't felt as bad as this ever that I can remember. I think looking after Esther all those years I felt I couldn't ever be ill as she needed me every day to see to her needs," Clive said.

As he was talking I got up, found a glass and poured Clive a generous measure of the brandy I'd bought.

"Here, Clive – drink this. It'll help, I think – at least, it will warm you up."

He didn't argue, but took the glass from me – gladly, I thought – and sipped away quietly.

"Clive, don't you think you should see a doctor?"

"Oh no, no need for that. I wouldn't know who to see, anyway. I'm not registered with anyone. It must be twenty years since I visited a doctor's surgery," Clive told me.

"But you must have needed a doctor for Esther on occasions?"

"No, Esther would never see a doctor. She always said I could meet her every need, and that's how it was," Clive said.

"Nevertheless it wouldn't hurt to have a check-up with somebody, Clive, and you should be registered with a doctor, you know."

"I'll think about it, Martha. I suppose you're right as usual, though I'm feeling a lot better for seeing you, my dear."

"I don't suppose you fancy a snack?"

"No, definitely not at the moment. I just feel so thirsty all the time though."

"Right – kettle on, cup of tea," I said, and I went into the kitchen.

I had just filled the kettle and switched it on when I smelled it: violets! It was faint at first, and then it became stronger, coming from above me somewhere. I looked up and there it was: a perfume bottle lying on its side, no top on it, with a drop of liquid gathering weight, and then it plopped down at my feet on the cold floor. A few seconds later another drop fell. I reached up to the shelf and took hold of the bottle. It was a largish bottle for a perfume bottle, I thought. I read on the front, 'African Violets'. A shiver went through me as I thought of Esther again! She hadn't left this house – a part of her was still here. Maybe it always will be.

The kettle switch went off with a loud click to tell me the water had boiled. This took my mind off Esther and the violets perfume, temporarily at least. I made the tea, let it brew a moment then poured out two mugs – one for Clive and one for me.

"Here you are, Clive – nice and hot."

I put the mug down on the small table between us. I felt Clive's hands – they were so cold. I held them tight, rubbing them briskly.

"I'm afraid I'm poor company just now," Clive said. "You know, up till this morning I'd lost my sense of smell for some reason, but I can smell some kind of perfume in here now."

"I know, Clive. It's African Violets perfume. I found a bottle of it on the kitchen shelf. The bottle was on its side and dripping a drop now and again on to the floor. Oh, Clive, I don't like it. It reminds me of— of . . ." I stuttered.

"Of Esther," Clive said.

"Yes, of Esther, but I thought you'd got rid of everything belonging to her."

"I thought I had, Martha. God knows what that perfume bottle was doing there. I didn't put it there. I am certain that shelf was cleared."

"Somebody put it there," I said.

We both kept silent for a while. I drank my tea and began to feel a little more at ease. If Clive and I are going to get edgy every time any little thing comes along to remind us of Esther, well, we'll never cope – with ourselves or with one another.

"Clive, it's so cosy in here. I wish I could stay and look after you, but I suppose I must be getting back to Jim."

"I wish you could stay here too, Martha. We're so very right for one another. Call it chemistry, fatal attraction . . . call it what you will, but it's there, it's real. Surely this is meant to be. It cannot be stifled – it is too strong for that," Clive said. He held my hands tightly in his as he spoke.

"Clive, you've gone all lyrical."

"Don't laugh at me, Martha – please don't. I'm deadly serious. I do so love you above anything and anyone. Martha, I believe our love is God-given. Surely He cannot give us such love for it just to be taken away? He could not be so cruel – a God who is just, a God who is kind. He would not taunt us and take our chance of happiness away by putting too many difficulties in the way – not a God of mercy." Such brave words from Clive!

"Stop it, stop it, Clive. Do not call on God in our cause. We have sinned grievously, taken a life He gave! It was not for us to play God and end that life. I know I did not kill her, but I am as guilty as you in God's eyes!"

I burst into tears as I'd done once or twice before in front of Clive. I can't ever recall crying in front of Jim. Clive comforted me, holding me close and wiping away my tears.

"Martha darling, please don't cry. It hurts me to see you so upset. Please don't be so distressed. All this will pass. You'll see – we'll win through. Believe it. We will, my darling – have faith!"

And we kissed hungrily, drinking in the feelings our love released, gluttoning the fever of the moment lest it be lost for ever. In that moment I felt I was a being apart, not of this earth, weightless – a free spirit. I can almost imagine it might be like this passing from this life to the next, so maybe death is not so fearsome after all? And all of this went through my mind in the space of a few seconds – incredible!

I released myself from Clive's tight hold with something of a push. I felt flushed and excited and not in control. I recovered my composure and knew I must go – no second thoughts. My heart was beating too quickly for my own good. I felt so many different emotions in such a short space of time. It was all too much for me. I wasn't used to such feelings – definitely not where Jim was concerned, not even when he was in his right mind.

It was Clive who interrupted my thoughts for he asked, "Martha, what's troubling you? You're not going? Please stay a little longer."

"No, Clive, I can't. I'm going. Don't ask me to stay. I'll see you tomorrow. No, it's not you, Clive; it's just that I . . . Oh, take no notice of me. I know I have some funny ways at times, but I can't help it. That's just me. No, it's nothing you've said or done. Forget it. It's you I am worried about. I can see you're not your usual self."

"The only time I'll be that, Martha, is when I can be sure we'll be together for good, but if you must go [and here he pulled me to him, holding me close as we embraced once more], then goodnight, my love."

I broke away from him and hurried back to my house. I stood in the kitchen a moment collecting my thoughts, and then I heard it: a low moaning noise. It came from upstairs. Jim! I'd not left him alone for so long before. I had been out most of the day, I recollected. I made for the stairs, increasing my pace as I reached the top. I could hear my heart beating. It was very fast and I could feel the pressure of blood running through my temples. I felt half afraid, as if I was about to experience something quite dreadful. I stopped a second outside Jim's room, took a deep breath and then went in.

And there he was – Jim. He was sitting, not in his own chair, but in the one opposite – the one Clive had been directed to on his visit to Jim. He was crying and the uncontrollable slavering had started again. All of a sudden I felt sorry for Jim. He made such a pathetic figure sitting there, his head half bowed, moaning spasmodically as if in a torment of mind, rather than of body.

"Jim, what is wrong? Are you ill? Why are you so upset?" I asked.

I'd gone across to him and put a comforting arm round his shoulders. He raised his head a little, pointing with an unsteady hand towards the chair he usually occupied.

"Look, Martha – look. He's gone. He's left us. Why did you send him away? Why?" Jim asked.

I couldn't make head nor tail of what he meant.

"Jim, who is it I'm supposed to have sent away?"

"You know who. You know. You did it!" Jim cried.

"Who, Jim? Tell me his name, for goodness' sake."

"It was Jim – poor, poor Jim. After all these years – gone, and he'll never come back. Why did you kill him, Martha? Why? What harm did he do you?" And Jim lowered his head into his hands and sobbed fitfully.

I could see it would be no good trying to reason with him. He was past all that at present – completely out of his mind again. No wonder he was certified insane all those years ago! He was getting worse. Fair enough, he appears more or less normal a lot of the time, but it is never maintained. His insanity was never more evident than at this moment.

"Look, Jim – why don't you sit over there in your own chair?"

"Oh yes, you'd like that, wouldn't you? You'd like me to take Jim's place. Well, I won't!" And Jim fell to moaning softly again, rocking slightly, head in hands.

I decided to leave him to get over it – whatever *it* was that caused him such anguish. A little while later I saw that Jim had his medication and went to his bed. I went to mine shortly after. Maybe he'll be in a better frame of mind tomorrow. I noticed that he hasn't even touched the tray of food I left him earlier in the day.

Chapter 37

"I've just come to warn you, dear: it's happened to me now! I don't know what this area is coming to, I really don't."

Yes, Mrs Jackson. It was half past eight in the morning too. I'd only just nicely got up and dressed.

"What is it that's happened to you, Mrs Jackson?" I asked.

"Rats, dear! Rats! Oh my, I nearly died of heart failure, I can tell you. I heard this scratching in the kitchen just before I went to bed last night. Well, I thought it might have been next door's cat – it gets in sometimes. I feed it bits, you know, so I thought it must be the cat scratching to get out. Anyway, I couldn't stand it any longer, so I went downstairs, didn't I? I didn't put the kitchen light on. Well, there was plenty of light from the hall, you see, and I was only going to open the back door to let Timmy out. That's the cat's name, dear – Timmy. But of course it wasn't Timmy scratching, was it, dear? And it was then I saw it – saw it looking at me! The light caught its eyes. It was nearly as big as a cat. It was a rat all right – a king-size rat! I thought it was going to spring at me. Oh, I was petrified. It was sitting looking at me from the top of the kitchen cupboard.

I unbolted the back door. I don't know how I managed it, dear. I was all of a tremble, and then I turned round and it was gone! It had disappeared, but where was it now? I felt it was still watching me from somewhere in the dark. I stood frozen where I was. After what seemed ages I saw a dark shape dive past me, out of the back door and into the garden. I shut and bolted the back door double quick! Oh, what an experience, dear! It was terrible!"

She sat down for several seconds to get her breath.

"How absolutely awful! I think you were very brave, Mrs Jackson, I really do" I said. "I don't know how I'd have coped, I'm sure."

"Well, dear, you just do, don't you? I've heard other neighbours say they've seen an enormous rat or two round here, but I thought they were exaggerating. I'll never doubt them again. Something's got to be done about this."

"I hear there've been mice about too since they demolished the old flour mill down the embankment. It can hardly be healthy for any of us. We'll have to get on to the Pest Control people again."

"Why? Have they been round here before?" Mrs Jackson enquired.

"Oh yes, they've been on my side of the road twice recently – well, ever since Mr Yately, next but one to me, complained he'd seen a rat in his back garden and Mrs Morgan, further up the road, rang the Pest Control people about finding mouse droppings in her kitchen cupboards. That's when I bought some stuff myself to put down just in case."

"You never mentioned that to me before, dear."

"Didn't I? Well, I was going to ring Pest Control myself, but I didn't get on with it. I think I will now – especially after the awful experience you've had!" I said.

"I'm certainly going to contact them," Mrs Jackson said. "I mean, you can't put up with vermin, can you? When I hear what a clean, desirable area this was when it was first built many, many years ago, and now it really has gone downhill, one way and another. But tell me, dear: is that stuff any good you bought to keep the place free from vermin?"

"Well, actually I bought rat poison, though I believe it works for any vermin," I told her.

"Could you give me a bit to try myself? I'll sprinkle it round the back-door area."

"You're welcome to try it, Mrs Jackson, but I think you'd be wiser to get the Pest Control people round to use their stuff. After all, they are the experts. That's what I am going to do," I said.

"Yes, you're probably right there, dear. I'll do that, and of course you've got to look out for people's pets when using vermin killer," she said.

"You certainly have," I agreed.

"By the way, I was just wondering if Clive's noticed any rats or mice about? Poor man – he doesn't look a bit well. I don't know what can be ailing him, I'm sure. Anyway, must go, dear. By the way, I like your hairdo. It quite suits you. You should have it done more often, dear. Bye."

And she was gone!

I sat down to reflect on Mrs Jackson's escapade with the rat. Not very nice for her, I must say. I took a sip of my tea, but one was quite enough. It was stone cold. If there's one thing I cannot abide it is tea that's gone cold. The cream of the milk had broken into fatty globules, giving a patchy surface to the tea – reminiscent of a stagnant pool, it occurred to me. No, even less now could I contemplate drinking that! I refilled the kettle and started afresh. Five minutes later I was on my way up to Jim with a cup of tea and some toast.

He used to want only tea in the morning, but of late he's asked for toast. I am glad of that as his appetite has been failing somewhat over the past few weeks. Any little extra he fancies must be a bonus. His appetite fluctuates, depending on his moods.

I wondered if he'd be in a better frame of mind this morning. He'd certainly been most strange last night. Well, I needn't have worried – he was almost his old self again. I'll rephrase that: he was almost his near-normal self again. He even smiled at me and asked me to stay. He didn't appear in the least to remember how upset he'd been only the night before. Still, I expect that's all part of the state of insanity. He may be said to gain something there over us 'sane' people, for we do not forget our upsets quite so easily!

I sat there quietly while Jim had his tea and toast.

When he'd dabbed up the remaining crumbs of toast with his moistened forefinger, he said, "Martha, listen to me – there's one or two things we've got to get straight between us, so hear me out."

And that did surprise me – Jim speaking so coherently first thing in the morning. His speech is usually very poor early in the day.

"Yes, Jim, and what is it we've got to get sorted out, then?" I asked.

He took a final swig at his tea, then he said, "I know – don't think I don't. I know what you've been up to, Martha, all these past months. You can't fool me. I know you too well! Oh yes, oh yes!" And he started his maniacal laugh again, as if the whole thing afforded him great amusement.

I couldn't help wondering what was coming next, and I was hoping my expression wasn't giving anything of my real thoughts away. What goings-on was Jim referring to? He must mean me and Clive, but that could hardly be described as 'goings-on'; and even if it was that, it is nothing to do with Jim. He doesn't own me. I am a free agent as regards whom I concern myself with, so what was I worrying about? It's funny how you can think of so much in what seems like a split second. Well, they do say 'quick as thought', don't they? They're right. And that's another thing – who are *they*? Nobody seems to know the answer to that one.

"No, Jim, I can't fool you. You're too clever for me by far," I said.

It usually pleases him no end if you let him think he is in the right and that he holds the winning hand over you.

"That's right, my girl – I'm glad you realise that. I don't mind, you know. Why should I? But there's the point about justice, you see. Hm, justice – that's the thing. The scales don't balance, Martha, so what are you going to do about it, eh?" Jim asked.

"Well, there's only one thing to do if the scales don't balance."

"What's that, then, Martha?"

"Why, get a new set of scales, Jim."

Oh, how he laughed at that! You'd have thought I'd just told him the greatest joke in the world.

"Get new ones! Oh, that's a good one, that is. Trust you, Martha, to think of that. Get new ones!"

Jim went on laughing, going more purple in the face by the minute, and then he stopped laughing as suddenly as he had started and his mood changed completely. He went dead quiet and stared straight in front of him, fixing his gaze on something which evidently I could not see; but whatever it was, it transfixed him all right for some time to follow as well. I picked up his cup and plate and left him to whatever it was that he was contemplating.

I couldn't help wondering as I walked downstairs what was really going on in Jim's mind? I had that uneasy feeling again – a foreboding of mishap. I'd had it before, but this time the feeling was much stronger, accompanied by a sense of urgency to be watchful of some hidden danger! Yet I had no idea what I was supposed to be looking out for. One thing was for sure: I mustn't let it get to me, whatever *it* might be. Knowing Jim, he'd probably have forgotten by tomorrow what he'd said today. He is like that.

Just then the phone rang.

"Hello. Yes, that's right. Oh, you will? Yes, this afternoon between two and three o'clock, you say? Very well, I'll be here. Yes, I suppose it is a must. I'll expect you then. Thank you. Goodbye."

It was the Pest Control people – funny that, because I had intended to contact them, but they got to me first. I wasn't intending going out today, so a visit from the Pest Control people was no problem.

I decided I would use my time to give the kitchen a good clean, for it certainly needed it and it would take my thoughts off Jim for a bit. I'd just finished washing down all the kitchen surfaces when the doorbell rang. I peeled off my rubber gloves, straightened my skirt and answered the door.

"From Floriana for Martha Madam," said a rosy-cheeked girl of about eighteen.

"Oh, that must be for me. Red roses – how beautiful!" I said, trying to look very surprised.

"Glad you're pleased, madam."

And off she went to do her next delivery, I suppose. I stood there admiring the roses. Beautifully presented, they were. I savoured the moment. I dallied at the front door, for I could see Mrs Jackson at her bedroom window peeping out to see what had been delivered to me. Well, the bouquet would set her wondering, I knew. I turned slowly and went indoors, closing the door quietly behind me.

So what if I bought and sent the roses to myself? I couldn't be more pleased if the Crown Prince of wherever had sent them! No, I couldn't, I am perfectly certain of that. But of course if they had come from Clive, well, that might be a different kettle of fish!

I went into the kitchen and got out my best cut-glass vase – the one I had never used in case some harm should befall it. It had been given to Jim and me as a wedding present by his Great-Aunt Ada all those years ago. We'd had several wedding presents, but had returned most of them as no wedding took place. It seemed the right thing to do in view of the way things had turned out. I can't remember why this vase was never returned. Anyway, beautiful roses deserve a beautiful container, and I had just that.

I undid the lace-patterned paper carefully, and the roses began to spread their volume amid the pretty green fernery. And then a smaller posy fell out near the base of the wrapping. I bent down slowly to pick it up – a small, neat and highly perfumed posy of tightly packed African violets! It was just like the scent of Esther when I moved her body, and just like the perfume her twin sister, Rachel, had worn, and just like the scent of the drips from the perfume bottle in Clive's kitchen. And now this. The scent was here with me in my kitchen, in my house! I felt Esther's presence near me somehow, and a cold shiver went down my spine!

It was twelve red roses I had ordered, so why the extra posy? I told myself it must be some 'free offer' which customers get if they spend over a certain amount of money. One or two shops have taken to doing that kind of thing lately, I know – just another way to boost sales, I guess.

I looked in the cupboard and found a small, squat vase. I put the violets in there and placed them on the kitchen window sill. The roses I put in the centre of the hall table. They look rich against the mahogany background. I put the delivery card in a prominent position on the table so I might read it each time I pass: 'To Martha with love'. Silly, I know, but it seemed to add a little something special to the day.

I didn't bother any further with cleaning the kitchen. Once interrupted, I lost heart. I tend to be like that. I can remember my old teacher at school – she was always criticising me for work unfinished.

"Perseverance, dear – that's what is required. Perseverance, my dear!" She said that often enough.

It seeped through to my annual reports even. I expect she was right too. It is only of late that I've got so very bad at starting things and not finishing them. These changes coincided with my meeting Clive.

Poor Clive! I'm not blaming him. I wonder how he is. He really isn't at all well just now. I often wonder how things will turn out for us in the future. There's days when it seems rosy enough, and then there's days when I almost wish we had never met. No, no, I don't mean that! I know now I'll never be the same if Clive goes out of my life completely.

"What are you waiting for?" I hear you ask.

Well, it's not as easy as that. Maybe if there was no Jim! But there is, and I've got to keep up this charade I started. I can't just walk out on him. Then there are the doctors who have kept my secret. Then there's Clive's wife – you see, it's complicated. The wages of sin . . . There's something in that too. You can tell I'm a clergyman's daughter, can't you? I was well grounded even if I've fallen away from my religion since. It never leaves you entirely though. I can understand how Clive came to do what he did. I can nearly understand why I helped him after Esther died. But if all comes to light, how will the world judge us? How would it all stand up in a courtroom? No, things are very far from straightforward. What am I waiting for? Need you ask?

***

Later that morning I went to see Clive. I went in by the back door. I could hear him in the kitchen. He was dressed, so I thought perhaps he was feeling a bit better.

"Martha – great to see you."

And we hugged one another for a few seconds.

"Clive, you do look a lot better today. Do you feel it?" I asked.

"I believe I do. Whatever it was seems almost to have left me. I just get a violent stomach pain now and then, but nothing like when I first started being ill, thank God. I've even kept a cup of tea down this morning, er, so far!"

"I still think you should see a doctor, Clive, for a check-up, just to be sure you're OK."

"Nonsense! You're all the tonic I need, Martha."

We went on into the lounge. It was lovely and warm in there with the gas fire full on.

"Martha, I've done a bit of thinking about things," Clive said.

"What things?" I asked.

"Oh, this and that."

"About us, do you mean?"

"Yes, that too, but I've been thinking about everything – the whole set-up: you, me, Esther, what's happened, Jim . . ." said Clive. "And I've decided it's high time we did something positive. We can't keep on like this, can we?"

"I don't see we can do anything about anything at present, Clive. It's still too near what happened here, in this house, to do anything which might, even remotely, raise suspicions about either of us. Oh, Clive, I don't know how you can bear to live here after what happened," I said.

"It would look peculiar if I move out suddenly, I should have thought."

"It might have done at first, but most people would feel they had to leave here – here in the place where – where . . ." I stammered.

"Go on, Martha, say it: where someone has been murdered! Yes, some would feel that, but I don't mind much in one way as I do feel Esther is still here watching me," Clive said.

133

"Clive, don't – don't say such things. How can she still be here? It's too horrible!" And I became quite distressed.

"Please, Martha, don't get so upset. You misunderstand. I like to believe Esther is still here, watching me, watching us when you are here. I like to think she can see how happy we make each other. She and I never made one another happy. I think she will only know now what she lost, what she destroyed day by day with her constant tongue-lashing outbursts of abuse. This house was a place of great unhappiness and, at times, deep despair. But you, Martha, turn it into a place of hope and love! That's why, Martha, we must make plans to hold on to this chance we've been given – this love of ours – to be happy whatever the difficulties. What do you say, my love?"

"You make it seem so easy, Clive, but it's only a pipe dream at present. I love you dearly and I know you love me, and if that were all that has to be considered there'd be no problem, but in our case things are not like that. You know that as well as I do, Clive. What would I do about Jim, for one thing?"

"I've been thinking about that too," Clive said. "You know, I think I ought to get to know Jim a bit better – get him into my confidence. We got on well enough when I first met him, didn't we? And he did ask me to visit again. What do you think, Martha?"

"Listen, Clive – there's a lot you don't know about Jim, or about me, or about what went on before I met you. I think it's time you were told," I said.

"Martha, you're sounding quite sinister. What's the big, dark secret, then?"

It was obvious I'd aroused his curiosity.

"Look – all this will take some time to explain. I'll come over tonight after I've seen Jim to bed. I'll double his sleeping pills so I know he'll stay asleep, and I'll be over about ten thirty, Clive."

"Fine by me."

"Trust me, Clive, there's a lot to tell!"

With this parting remark, I left and went home. It would be nice to have someone near me to share my secrets with, but I've had to keep things to myself for safety's sake – Jim's and mine, that is. There is my sister, Ruth, of course, but she wouldn't tell anyone about what happened to Jim. I'd trust her with my life. I feel Clive will understand when I explain everything; and if I can't confide in him, then who can I confide in? He's trusted me all right. There is one person, not a million miles away, I'll never take into my confidence. You know who, don't you? Yes, you're right – Mrs Jackson. She is a good person to speak to though if I ever want some news spreading around. Mind you, it might bear very little similarity at all to the original version, but that is a risk you take when dealing with Mrs J!

I took Jim a bit of lunch up – some soup and a crusty roll. He was quiet and merely nodded the lunch tray in the direction of the small table next to his chair. He started on his soup at once and ignored me, so I left him to it. I went downstairs and had the rest of the soup myself. Then I washed a few bits up and made a start on the ironing. I've been a bit lax of late, and the pile of ironing had got rather out of hand. I felt angry with myself for letting it get so. Still, it wouldn't go away so I decided I'd better get on with it. I was just beginning the seventh shirt when there was a ring at the door. It provided a welcome relief from the monotony of my chores.

It was only one o'clock, but it was the men from Pest Control. On the phone they had said they would come between two and three o'clock, so they'd come early – not that it made any difference to me.

"Sorry we're a bit early, madam, but we finished our other calls sooner than expected," said one of the two men at the door.

"Oh, that's no problem. Come in," I said.

The shorter man entered first, carrying a kind of bucket and a stirrup pump. He was followed by an extremely thin, taller man who carried a briefcase.

"May we have your help first of all, for a few moments, answering our questionnaire?" asked the taller of the two men as he took some papers from his briefcase.

"Of course. Here – take a seat at the kitchen table. Just pull the stools out – there you are," I said.

The questionnaire was pretty general, asking if I'd seen any vermin around and so on. Also had I put any vermin killer down myself? Yes, I had. Could they see the stuff? Look as I would, I couldn't find the poison I had bought. I'd put it in the shed, but it wasn't there.

"I'm sorry – I can't seem to find it at the moment," I told the men.

"No problem, madam. We have our own special stuff here we use. If you find yours, either dispose of it safely or give it to us and we will deal with it; but meanwhile, we will use our own products."

They asked permission to place their poison around the back garden at strategic points, which they indeed did, also spraying a solution from the stirrup pump in various places. When they had finished they said they would be back in two weeks to check if any progress had been made. They said people in the area had been most co-operative.

I thanked them for their help and then they left to visit the house next door.

Chapter 38

It was after ten thirty when I got over to Clive's that evening. He had set the side table out with dainty sandwiches, pastry bits and drinks. I saw he had my favourite drink there: cherry brandy liqueur. It was a new bottle. All the years with Jim I had hardly ever tasted any alcohol, and yet with Clive I'd been treated to a variety of drinks.

"I thought you weren't coming," Clive said. "Every visit from you is a bonus, you know."

"Honestly, Clive, you talk as if I'm a ration portioned out at intervals," I said, laughing.

"Well, you must admit, my dear Martha, our meetings are a bit spasmodic; but I appreciate now that absence does make the heart grow fonder," Clive said.

"Don't worry, Clive – it surely won't always be like this, one day. Anyway, what I'm here for could take some time, as I told you earlier."

"In that case, let's get comfortable and start with some liquid refreshment. Cherry brandy?"

"Perfect choice, Clive – just perfect," I said. "You know, Clive, I'll have to stop this drinking habit I seem to have fallen into since meeting you. You'll be turning me into an alcoholic if I don't watch it!"

"I can't see that happening to you, Martha."

I smiled and took a sip or two of my drink. Then, feeling somewhat renewed, I began the task of unfolding my secrets of many years. First I filled Clive in on all the background of what I needed to tell him. With one or two pauses it took me over thirty minutes before I'd said what I wanted Clive to know.

He was very quiet for a while and seemed lost for words at first about what to say to all that I had told him.

"Well, come on, Clive – you must have something to say, surely?"

"Of course I have, but you've quite taken my breath away! It's just the unbelievable situation you set up so long ago and how it's all held together. It's truly amazing – there's no other word to describe it. But then, I knew from the moment I met you that you are no ordinary person. I sensed there was something very different about you – very different from anyone else I had ever known. How right that has proved to be, in so many ways. You know what I admire most of all about you is your devotion to Jim. It's obvious you must have loved him in the beginning. Your determination to keep him from a lifetime in a mental home – very few people could have contrived matters the way you have, Martha. Amazing – truly amazing!"

"As I explained, Clive, I felt I owed Jim at least the chance of a different life from that of being confined for life in a mental institution. And you're right, I did love Jim once, but that Jim disappeared from the face of the earth; and now, for the past ten years, I've been left with a very different Jim – a man whose mind has been damaged beyond repair. Now my feelings towards that man are nothing more than compassion and sadness towards a fellow human being in his suffering. What I feel for you, Clive, is very different indeed. It's a feeling of wishing to be totally committed to your happiness and well-being forever. And there you have it, Clive. Now you know all my secrets. All is revealed, as they say. So what do you think of your Martha now?"

"Come here, closer to me, and I'll show you what I think of you, my dearest love."

We embraced for a long moment as Clive smoothed his lips along my cheek, resting them by my ear to tell me once more how much he loves me. Such moments have become so precious to me, but all too often I am apt to cut them short with cold, sobering thoughts which bring me back to reality. I had one such thought at that particular juncture.

I told Clive, "We're behaving like a couple of teenagers, newly in love."

"So? Why shouldn't we? Long may we feel like this! I know what you need, Martha – a refill."

I raised no objection. We talked long into the night about how we could achieve a future together. It was after one o'clock when I left Clive.

I looked up at the bedroom windows as I reached home, and there it was: a light on in the spare room, the room where Jim did his carpentry.

'Surely,' I thought, 'he can't be in there now'

Impossible! He had a double dose of sleeping tablets. I'd seen him take them. At least I'd watched him apparently throw four – instead of the usual two – into his mouth. He'd put his cupped hand to his mouth followed by a drink of water. Yes, of course he'd taken his pills. And yet the light? I decided to go and investigate.

I went upstairs very quietly. I turned the handle of the spare- room door, but it wouldn't open – it was locked. I could see the light still on in there from the crack under the door. Next I went into Jim's room.

Yes, there he was, flat on his back, snoring intermittently.

'Oh well,' I thought, 'he must have been in the spare room before he got into bed. He must have left the light on, come out and locked the door. I'll get the key from him in the morning, unlock the door and turn the light off.'

I went to bed and fell asleep almost at once.

Chapter 39

Next day I was up rather later than usual. I'd slept very heavily. Must have been the alcohol! I couldn't recall my dreams clearly, but I knew they'd been troubled ones – all about being late and missing things I was supposed to attend. I had a quick wash and brush-up and went down to put the kettle on. My mouth was so dry in the mornings. I couldn't understand why. I'd never had this trouble until recently. I felt much more civilised after the first cup of tea. I was just about to pour a second when I heard a kind of singing from upstairs. I went to listen. Yes, I was right: it was Jim, half singing, half humming some old tune or other.

'He must be feeling more cheerful at any rate,' I thought.

I took a cup of tea up to him. As I passed the spare-room door I saw the light was no longer on.

"Morning, Jim. Nice cup of tea for you. You're in a good mood today," I said.

"Of course I am, Martha. I've good reason to be too." And Jim chuckled away to himself.

"What's pleasing you so much, Jim? What's happened?" I asked.

"Oh, it's not what has happened," said Jim. "It's what's going to happen."

"Is that a fact? And what's going to happen, Jim? Something interesting?"

"Ah, now, that would be telling, wouldn't it just?" Jim said in a tantalising tone.

I didn't pursue the enquiry. It was probably just one of Jim's funny moments and nothing more would come of it.

"Would you like some breakfast, Jim?"

"Yes, Martha, I think I would. Now, what shall I have, eh?" Jim pondered.

I felt I should have been passing him a menu to look at. Maybe he thought he was in a café – you never know!

"Toast and marmalade?" I suggested. "You usually like that, Jim."

"No, no, I want a proper breakfast today. I need nourishment, you see, for what I've got to do; so I'll have a cooked breakfast. Yes, I'll have eggs and bacon and fried tomatoes and fried bread. Oh yes, and a couple of sausages. Yes, that will do nicely," Jim said.

"I should just think it will, Jim. My goodness, when did you last ask for such a breakfast, Jim? You can spring a surprise when you want to," I said.

"You just wait, Martha. I haven't even started springing surprises yet, my girl. There's bigger surprises than this to come, I can promise you – oh yes, much bigger." And Jim gave out his maniacal laugh once more.

I went into the kitchen and set about making Jim his breakfast. It is strange to have the smell of bacon cooking in the morning in our house. I hadn't made a breakfast like that for Jim in the last five years. I decided I might as well include myself in this 'feast', and threw two more bacon rashers and sausages into the mix.

It is fortunate I had some sausages and bacon available as I don't often buy them these days.

Soon Jim was tucking in happily to his breakfast. What a plateful, but he demolished the lot! He even said he enjoyed it.

I went downstairs, took my breakfast from under the grill, where I'd been keeping it warm, sat down at the kitchen table and began my meal. I must say that though I don't usually indulge in a cooked breakfast I did enjoy this one. It was only after I'd had a second cup of tea and two pieces of toast that I realised I'd gone too far with the eating. I felt so very full – 'bloated', as my mother used to say.

I had intended having a good clean of the lounge today, but after such a breakfast I felt more like going back to bed and sleeping it off. I began to feel quite disgusted with myself for being so greedy!

Lethargically, I cleared the table and set about washing up. I was so slow and making heavy weather of it.

'I'd better bring Jim's pots down,' I thought.

Strange to say, when I got up there Jim had done a most unusual thing: he'd packed up his dirty dishes all neatly on his tray ready for me to take away. He'd never done such a thing before. He must have a bit more thought than I had been giving him credit for. He even put his serviette on top of the plates. I did notice the tray was unusually heavy though as I carried it downstairs.

And then I saw it! As I removed the serviette I saw it on Jim's plate and I nearly fainted at the sight! I dropped the tray, which crashed to the floor. I was too shocked to utter a sound at first, but a few seconds later I let out the most awful scream, for there, on Jim's plate, was a medium-sized dead rat! I was terrified! How had it got there?

I wanted to get rid of it at once, but I daren't touch it. I left it and ran upstairs to Jim.

"Jim! Jim! Oh, my God, Jim, there was a dead rat on your tray!" I yelled hysterically.

Jim roared and laughed so much I thought he would have a fit. He said "I know, I know. I put it there. Isn't it good, Martha? You see, it works. I knew it would!" And he burst into another round of laughter.

I could see I'd get no sense out of him in this mood.

Just as I was about to go downstairs Jim called me back to ask if I could get his radio out of the spare room. He'd left it in there. I went to collect it and got another shock. The tin of rat poison I had bought was there on the floor by the radio! I'm sure I never left it there!

Back in the kitchen, I took an old towel and threw it over the thing on the floor. I knew that didn't solve the problem and that I'd have to get rid of it sooner or later, but I was too petrified to do anything else at that moment. I've had a horror of rats all my life – more than most people. Most other creatures I don't mind, even spiders. In fact, I'm quite fond of them – especially the furry-legged variety. Now, as for Mrs Jackson, seeing furry spiders – or any other spiders, for that matter – would just about finish her off, or so she's always led me to believe.

I remember she once asked me to go to her house and lift a spider from her doorstep before she dared go in. I hadn't minded that a bit, but rats . . . I definitely draw the line there. Rats suggest some kind of evil to me somehow. I'll have to get a tremendous amount of courage up before I can remove that rat, I know. Maybe I'll ask Clive to do it. I'll see.

What did Jim mean by saying he put it there and that it works? What works? I am beginning to get that uneasy feeling again about Jim and whatever he gets up to at times.

I think if I'd won the pools this morning it would have been knocked out of my mind by the rat experience! Just as I was calming down there was a ring at the doorbell, and who should it be but the tall man from Pest Control.

"Sorry to trouble you, madam, but you didn't by any chance find a Yale key around here after my last visit?" he enquired.

"Er, no, I'm sorry – I didn't," I told him.

"I'm checking all the visits I made in case I dropped it somewhere," he said.

"Sorry – I can't help you there."

And he turned to go.

"Oh, please, just a minute – don't go. I was wondering if you could help me. You see, I had a rather upsetting experience earlier on."

I must have appeared scared, as the man looked somewhat concerned.

"Certainly, madam. If I can be of any assistance I'll be only too pleased to help. What is the problem?" he enquired.

"Come into the kitchen."

He followed me in.

"Take a look there under that old towel on the floor."

He walked over and slowly lifted one end of the towel. He paused with the towel half-raised, turned round to look at me, gave a low whistle between his teeth and whipped the whole towel away to reveal the dead rat.

I must have disturbed it putting the towel over it, and it was now lying on its side with glazed eyes staring. Its eyes reminded me of old dogs' eyes when they're going blind.

"My God, lady, where did that come from?" he asked.

"I don't know. It just appeared on the plate, on the tray, dead, as you can see. Please, I'm so terrified of rats – even dead ones. Oh, please, could you dispose of it for me? I'd be most grateful."

"No problem, madam. In fact I'd be interested to take this specimen for examination and investigation. It looks like our rat-poison-laying sessions are beginning to pay off. Yes, indeed, this could be the first of many, though I hope you don't find any more in the house like this one."

"Oh, I can't thank you enough for removing it. I'm such a coward when it comes to rats, but I can't help it. Would you like a bin liner to put

143

it in? Look – put it in that old towel first, then. Here you are – take this garden refuse bag. It's quite thick and strong."

He did as I suggested.

"By the way, madam, did you ever find the rat poison you bought yourself?" he asked.

"Yes, I did. I'll get it for you." And I took it from the cupboard and handed it to him.

"I'm afraid there doesn't seem to be much left. I sprinkled it outdoors rather liberally." The tin of rat poison was the one I'd taken from the spare room.

"I'll take this tin and the deceased back with me to our lab and see what we can find out, if anything. It's lucky I happened to call on you today. Don't forget we'll be on our next official visit round here in just over a week, and we hope we'll have solved the vermin problem by then. Good morning, madam."

"Good morning and thank you." And I breathed a sigh of relief, I was so pleased at the rat's exit.

Next I took the plate the rat had been on and threw it in the bin. It was one of Jim's mother's plates – one of the few 'special' ones left, one of those I'd taken so much care of over the years. Well, it was gone now and there was an end to it – and the rat! I was certain I'd never fancy using, or even handling, that particular piece of crockery again! I didn't even fancy washing it up! I don't suppose Jim will miss it or even realise it was his mother's. It is his fault it's gone anyway. He must have put the rat on the plate for me to find, and he seems to think it was a big joke judging by the way he roared with laughter. Serves him right, then, if the plate's gone!

I hate the idea that the rat was scampering around upstairs before it died. Did poison kill it? Did Jim kill it? What if there are other rats in the house? I'm trying hard to dismiss such thoughts from my mind.

Chapter 40

It was Thursday – my usual day for doing my 'big' shop, but after checking my larder I realised there wasn't a lot I really needed. I always buy more than I know I will use. That is a bit of my mother's philosophy rubbing off on me. 'Always put something by for a rainy day' – that's what she said and what she used to instil into me. Well, I've always followed her advice on that one. Still, if I don't need much shopping I think I'll still go off to town. I'll feel better if I only look round the shops and have a coffee out after my rat encounter. Clive will probably be in town today as well.

I was soon ready to go.

'I know,' I thought, "I'll make an appointment at that posh hair salon I went to last time. Yes, I'll book a shampoo and blow-dry. Why not? I deserved to treat myself after the morning's upset. I didn't even bother to shout goodbye to Jim. I felt so annoyed with him for playing his sick-rat joke on me.

I left the house, making for the bus stop. I looked at my watch and knew a bus was about due, but – would you believe it? – the bus suddenly sailed past me before I reached the stop. I'd missed it and there wouldn't be another one for half an hour! Oh, what a nuisance and it was just starting to rain!

I was about to turn round and wait indoors until the time of the next bus when a voice called me. "Martha, Martha, here – over here."

It was Clive, I knew, but I couldn't see him anywhere. He called again and then I did see him. Actually he 'pipped' at me. I was quite astonished to see him sitting at the wheel of a car – a brand-new one too by the look of it! I ran across to him.

"Clive, what a surprise! I never thought of seeing you at the wheel of a car! Whose car is it, then?"

"Mine, my dear – all mine. How do you like it?"

I looked it over for a few seconds – midnight blue with a white stripe and lighter-blue upholstery. I didn't know what make it was – I hardly know one car from another.

"Clive, it's absolutely beautiful. Is it really yours? Truly?"

"Of course it's mine. I picked it up this morning," he said.

"You've never spoken before about getting a car, have you?"

"I thought I'd surprise you, Martha."

"Well, you've certainly done that, Clive."

"I've been thinking about getting transport for some time now. I did a bit of shopping around and then took the plunge, as they say."

"Well, you've chosen well. It's a lovely car, Clive, and it looks so posh!"

"Going to town, are we? Well, hop in and see what you think of the ride."

And I did just that.

"Lovely smooth ride, Clive," I said.

"I'm glad you approve. You see, Esther never wanted me to have a car. I used to have one, but she made me get rid of it. She had a horror of going out in cars – said she knew she'd be killed in one if she did. She'd once been involved in a bad crash. That was before I met her. It was injuries from that accident that left her progressively paralysed, ending up in a wheelchair before we'd been married for three years. She never went out after that. Well, you know how upset and hysterical she could be, so I gave in to her and that was the end of my driving – until now!"

It was the first time Clive had told me how Esther came to end up in a wheelchair, and we drove without speaking for a little while.

It was me who spoke first: "This lift is very handy, Clive, as I have just missed the bus."

"I know, my love. I saw it go by and that's why I was sitting in the car waiting for you. I only collected the car from the garage an hour ago, and I've done a few miles round about to get used to it. I feel quite at ease with it already."

"Are you going to the shops, Clive?"

"Yes, though I don't need much," he said.

"Neither do I, but I feel I need to get out of the house for a bit," I said.

There was a one-way system round the town with free car parks at the main shopping centre; and although it was quite busy, we managed to find a suitable place to stop. Clive locked the car and we made for the shops.

"I'll just slip in here and make an appointment, Clive."

It was my posh salon. It seemed somewhat smaller than on my first visit, but the girls were every bit as glamorous. I recognised the girl who had done my perm. She was behind the enquiry desk.

"Yes, modom, we could fit you in for a wash and blow-dry the day after tomorrow. That's Saturday at ten o'clock or two o'clock. Which time would modom prefer?" asked the assistant.

"The ten-o'clock appointment would be fine," I said.

She gave me a card with the appointment time on it.

"Thank you," I said, and left the shop.

"That was quick", Clive said, "for a hairdo."

"Don't be silly – I only made an appointment!"

"So you did. Only kidding! Where to now, Martha?" Clive asked.

"Nowhere in particular. I really only came out for a change. I was feeling a bit down, what with one thing and another."

"Why? What's gone wrong? Is it Jim?" Clive asked.

"Well, sort of," I said.

"Tell me about it."

"I will later. Just let me get some bread and a few bits from Maxi's," I said.

"Right – you do that. I've a couple of things to do myself. Look – how about if we meet in the Gardener's Arms in about half an hour in the lounge? We should both have got what we want by then. We could have a drink and a pub lunch," Clive said.

"Great! Let's do that. See you there, then."

Clive went about his business and I went about mine. I went to two or three shops and bought the necessaries plus a few extras. Funny how you do seem to buy more than you set out to get. I was beginning to feel the benefit of going out already, although I have to admit deep down it is because I'd met up with Clive on the way. He certainly had a therapeutic effect on me which no medication could ever supply.

I was longer than anticipated buying what I wanted as the shops were so busy. It was well over half an hour since leaving Clive when I actually caught up with him in the pub. I'd only been in there once before, and that was with Clive. It would never have occurred to me, before I met Clive, to go into a pub at all, especially on my own. I expect if Jim had been 'normal' and we'd been married, as first planned, then I'd have gone in with Jim. Jim used to be partial to a pint or two, years ago.

I couldn't see Clive at first, then he came towards me and led me to the table where he had been sitting.

"Sorry to be so long, Clive, but the shops I went in were so busy."

"No problem, Martha. It's given me time to look at the menu. What would you like?"

I scanned the menu and was surprised to see so many dishes on offer.

"Just a ploughman's, I think, Clive."

"Me too," he said. "Two ploughman's it is, then."

And off he went to order.

Clive was gone some time and I became aware of someone in the corner opposite staring at me rather pointedly and whispering. I gave a quick glance in that direction and saw it was some neighbours of mine – a Mr Jarvis and his wife. They averted their gaze when I looked up and fell to whispering again. I had the feeling they were talking about Clive and me. I could imagine what they were concocting too. I tried to ignore it, but I still felt uneasy for some reason.

"Here we are. I thought I might as well bring the food myself," Clive said. "That way I persuaded the waitress to double your cheese portion, Martha, as I know you're so fond of it!"

"Thanks, Clive. That was sweet of you."

Neither of us spoke for the next few minutes as we were busy tucking into our lunches. As I happened to look across from where I was sitting, I saw that the Jarvises had gone. I continued my eating in silence – silence, that is, except for the crackling noise as we bit into the crusty bread rolls that came with the ploughman's. You can hardly be ladylike eating that kind of thing. Clive was a faster eater than me – his plate was all but empty. But then, as he pointed out, I did have a double cheese portion to get through – and very palatable it was too.

"Fancy anything else?" Clive asked.

I gave a couple of quick chews and swallowed the rest of the cheese down before I could answer.

"Oh no, nothing more, Clive. That was very filling. But don't let me stop you having something more."

"Not for me either, Martha. As you say, it was quite filling, but I did enjoy it. But you haven't touched your drink yet, Martha. Do you know what I got you?" he asked.

"Yes, Clive, I think I do. You bought me this drink the last time we came here. It's a St Clement's, isn't it?"

"Absolutely right," Clive said. "Last time you praised it so highly I thought it would stand repeating."

"You couldn't have chosen better," I said. "Cheers, Clive! Here's to better days ahead!"

And we raised our glasses a fraction as Clive said, "I'll drink to that, Martha!"

"Time, ladies and gentlemen, please!"

That was the landlord, anxious to close for his afternoon siesta. Well, I suppose he's as entitled to his breaks as the rest of us.

"Clive, I think he means us – time to go. We're about the last ones in here."

We drank up and left.

"Where are you going, Martha? The car is this way," Clive said.

"Oh yes, I forgot. I was going to the bus stop, Clive."

"Well, that's nice, I must say. My brand-new car can't have made much impression on you after all!"

"Oh, Clive, it's not that; it just takes a bit of getting used to the idea, that's all. I didn't even know you could drive until today."

"Come on, Martha – this way. This is a short cut to where the car's parked."

We were soon in the car and away. The drive home seemed so much quicker than the trip out somehow. As I got out of the car the Jarvises (the people who'd eyed me in the pub) were just getting out of their car a few doors from Clive's house. They both took a good long look at me as I shut Clive's car door, and when I turned in their direction they both hurried down their garden path. Well, if they wanted to ignore me, that was up to them. They have always acknowledged me in the past. I turned round, said goodbye to Clive and went indoors. The house seemed uncannily quiet when I went in. I stood momentarily at the foot of the stairs and listened intently – for what? I couldn't say.

Jim usually had his radio on about this time of day. There was a daily serial on that he appeared to enjoy, but I couldn't hear any radio on at the moment. I never knew how much Jim understood of what he listened to on the radio, but often he thought of characters in plays as real people in real-life situations. I knew this to be so because he used to tell me about them. Once when an actor playing an old woman 'died' in one episode of a serial, Jim wanted me to send a floral tribute from him to her funeral. That's how real it all was to him.

I pretended to do it for him. I've always found it best to go along with him in such matters. It is never any good trying to explain the reality of such a situation to him. I think after all these years looking after Jim I'd get on well working in a mental home. Mind you, I don't think there will ever be any chance of me taking a job anywhere now. Jim's my full-time occupation, though I can't help wishing daily that it was Clive I was devoting my life to!

I made a pot of tea and had just put two cups on a tray with some fruit cake when I heard it – Jim's stick banging impatiently on the floor above.

"Coming, Jim! Just coming," I called, and I was on my way up the stairs.

I had to push Jim's door with my foot and hold the tray somewhat aloft to see what I was doing.

"Here we are, then, Jim – a nice cup of tea and your favourite fruit cake. How's that, now?"

"Starving, that's what I am – starving! Thank God you're here. It's 'er, you know. She's trying to kill me, but she won't. Oh no, she'll go first, you'll see!" Jim said, and he laughed his insane laugh as of old.

"That's right, Jim, nobody's going to get the better of you, are they? But tell me: who is trying to kill you? Do I know this person, Jim?" I asked.

"It's 'er – that woman who keeps me here a prisoner. It's that Martha. You must have seen 'er," Jim said.

"Oh, her! Don't worry about her, Jim. She's nobody. She can't hurt you – I won't let her. No, don't you bother yourself about her, Jim," I told him.

That seemed to calm him down a bit.

"I can listen to it now, you know," Jim said.

"Listen to what, Jim?"

"The radio, of course. Oh, she doesn't like it, you know – jealous, I shouldn't wonder. It's all because of that Ellen on the radio. I've taken to her in a big way, and I know that Martha woman is jealous of her. Now, what do you say to that, eh?"

"Oh, I wouldn't take any notice of that Martha if I were you, Jim. Here – I'll put your radio on for you. There now – you can listen to your serial and enjoy your tea and cake."

I left him and didn't bother to pour a cup of tea out for myself. Down in the kitchen I sat awhile pondering over what Jim had just said. His mind must be in a hell of a state.

I can't help wondering who Jim thinks I am – me, the person who has just taken his tea up to him. Trying to keep him prisoner, did he say? Wanting to kill him? Wherever did he get such ideas? He's had very mixed-up ideas about things for some time now. So long as he doesn't turn violent I'll probably be able to manage him for a long time yet. But this isn't getting Clive and me together any more quickly though. I despair sometimes of us ever making it.

Chapter 41

The phone rang. It was my sister, Ruth. She's taken to ringing me about once a fortnight now, usually on Fridays or Saturdays around eleven in the morning, but for some reason she'd chosen a different day this week. It was Monday at seven o'clock. She seldom talks for longer than five minutes or so, but this time proved a little different. She was not quite her normal self, it seemed to me. She was quite excited, in fact. Her talk was general at first, but then came the real reason for her call: she was getting MARRIED! In a month, in fact, to the gentleman she'd been corresponding with since that holiday of hers.

Well I never! Who'd have thought it? I wouldn't, for one. I'd never for one moment have imagined my sister getting married again – well, especially not now, at her age. I mean, she's – let me see, yes, she'll be forty-nine next month. I know she was very young when she first married, but when her husband died unexpectedly . . . Well, that seemed to be that as far as she was concerned; and she always said she'd never marry again even if the chance came about. So that is why I am so surprised by her news, but she certainly does appear to have taken to the gentleman in a big way. Charlie is his name.

I told Ruth, "It is all a bit sudden, isn't it?"

But she dismissed that and said these things are not really a matter of time. It can happen in a month, a week or a day if it is meant to. I could understand that when I thought about it later on. It hadn't taken Clive and me long to realise we had something very special indeed going on for us. Actually, I had never let my sister in on that particular piece of news. Maybe I would soon.

"Well, aren't you going to congratulate me, Martha?" my sister asked over the phone. "And of course you'll be at the wedding. I'll let you know all the details later. Charlie's getting a special licence, you know."

And apart from telling her I would be there, I did indeed congratulate her and Charlie on their forthcoming marriage. I had little more to say. Ruth had to ring off as she'd to go to work. She is a part-time receptionist at the health centre.

Well, well, talk about surprises! Go to the wedding? How could I? It was so far away and I couldn't take Jim, could I? He was dead and buried, wasn't he? There might be somebody up there who'd known him. That would give them a shock! And I couldn't leave Jim either. I'd have to wait and see.

That evening I was over at Clive's a bit earlier than usual. He was just making a cup of tea so we had one together. I'd taken him a fruit cake I'd made that morning. I know he is partial to fruit cake. Funny that – so is Jim.

"Can I cut a piece now?" Clive asked.

"Of course, Clive – it's yours. I made it specially for you."

He set about cutting a sizeable wedge. While he was eating the cake, I told him my latest news about Jim and his mixed-up thoughts and about my sister's forthcoming marriage.

"I'll tell you what, Martha," said Clive, having swallowed the last few crumbs of his cake. "I'll tell you what: you could go to your sister's wedding if I look after Jim for you. What do you think?"

"Oh, I don't think so, Clive. That would never work. Jim would have to be in a better state of mind for that, I'm afraid. He's so strange at the moment, like there's something sinister about to happen. I don't know what it is, but there's definitely something afoot," I said.

"Well, there's time yet, isn't there, Martha? Think about it though. I'd be only too willing to help out – you know that."

"I will, Clive, and it's nice of you to offer, but don't get your hopes up!"

I noticed Clive eyeing the rest of the cake.

"Go on – I know you want it. Cut yourself another piece, Clive."

And he did.

Meanwhile I helped myself to another cup of tea and gave Clive a refill.

"Have you heard from your brother, Clive, since he left here?"

"Funny you should mention that, Martha. Take that card off the table – it's from David. It came this morning," Clive told me. I picked up the card. It was very colourful with blue water and palm trees and exotic flowers growing.

"Go on – read it, Martha. It's not private. David never says much when he writes anyway."

And he was right. It merely said, 'Here on business. Will write more soon. Very busy schedule just now. Regards, David.' Yes, he really was a man of few words – on postcards, at any rate. But it was the postmark that caught my attention.

"Hawaii? Oh, Clive, isn't he the lucky one. I used to dream of going somewhere exotic one day, but it's a pretty silly thought now, I admit. I thought you said Clive was off to India to work when he left you?"

"He was, Martha, but now he's obviously moved on to Hawaii," Clive said.

"That must be some job David has," I remarked.

"It is Martha. He's done well for himself all right," Clive told me.

"What exactly does David do for a living?"

"David? He's had quite a few jobs in his time, but for the past five years he's been a co-director in a chemical firm in the States to do with crop-spraying and that sort of thing. He's the clever one in the family, David is – got his degree in business qualifications and God knows what else. With his present post he travels all over the world getting orders and such. Yes, David's been very successful in any job he's had. Mind you, this last one seems to be the best one of all, from both a financial and a job-satisfaction point of view. I'm afraid I've never achieved very much."

And Clive gave a deep sigh as if realizing he'd missed out on a great deal – compared to his successful brother anyway.

"Well, money isn't everything," I said, trying to cheer Clive a little. "And then you've had Esther to care for full-time, so you were handicapped as regards getting on in the world."

"Yes, I suppose I was, Martha. I'm not grumbling though. I've a great deal to be thankful for – most of all meeting you, my love."

"You're always telling me that, Clive!"

"That's because it's true and always will be, Martha."

"That's comforting to know, and it's the same for me knowing you; but then, I don't need to tell you that either," I said.

"Don't ever stop telling me, Martha. Don't ever change," Clive said.

"I won't ever. I promise."

The chiming of Clive's old grandfather clock brought me back to reality. Midnight! I must get back home. I kissed Clive and hurried away. Ten minutes later I was in my bed and I don't even remember falling asleep.

Chapter 42

I've had a visit from the Pest Control people this morning. They told me they were checking to see if there are any more signs of vermin in the area. I was glad to tell them I haven't seen any.

"That's good news, madam; and the neighbours tell me the same, I'm glad to say."

This information was from the tall Pest Control officer I'd seen the first time they came round – the one who so kindly removed the dead rat from my kitchen. I knew I'd be eternally grateful to him for that!

"So that's the end of the rat invasion, you think?" I asked.

"I hope so, madam, but there is one other matter I'm here for."

"And what's that, then?"

"You'll remember about the dead rat I took away from your kitchen?"

"Remember it? I'll never forget it!" I said with a shudder.

"Well, madam, we took that specimen to our laboratory for examination, and it turns out it died from poisoning all right; but it wasn't from the poison we use. We established what kind of poison it was, and no ordinary person would be able to buy it without signing the Dangerous Poisons Book. We think it died from the poison that you put down. Were you asked to sign for it when you bought it, madam?"

"No, I was not. It was sold to me just the same as I would purchase any other item in that shop," I told him. "I bought it from Hardwick's, the hardware shop in town."

"Right – we'll be paying them a visit to make a few enquiries."

"Does it matter much, then?"

"Yes, I'm afraid it does. For one thing, we don't want any unauthorised person buying such a substance and for another administering such a substance results in a most agonising death for the recipient, be it human or animal, madam."

"Oh dear," I said. "Much as I loathe rats, I wouldn't want them to die in agony."

"I'm sure you would not. Well, now that we've cleared the area and made it safe we'll be off."

"Oh, just a minute – I've got your bucket and stirrup pump here still."

"Oh yes, thank you. I'll take them away now. Good morning, madam."

When he'd gone I busied myself with the ironing. Half an hour later it was all done. I took it upstairs and put it away. I looked in on Jim. I saw he'd dozed off. He's been doing a lot of that lately.

***

Saturday came – hairdo day. I was looking forward to it. It wouldn't mean much to people who go regularly to the hairdresser's, but it was a great treat for me. Mrs Jackson obviously took it all as a matter of course, like all the other expensive ventures she pursued. They do say that familiarity breeds contempt. It will be some time, I reckon, before I need to let that worry me. I got ready and caught the nine-twenty bus to town. I went into a couple of shops first, then on to the salon. I checked in at the reception desk.

"Good morning, madam," said an assistant.

She was one I had not seen before – not quite so upmarket as the ones I'd met on my last visit. I was a 'madam' instead of a 'modom' today.

"A wash and blow-dry? Ah, yes, here we are, madam. Françoise will be attending you if you'd care to take a seat for a moment."

I was just about to sit down when a most pleasant, good-looking, tall girl approached me.

"Good morning. My name is Françoise. This way if you please."

I followed obediently.

All the girls had their names embroidered in gold on their white work suits. Two minutes later I was gowned and the shampooing began. I had really started to enjoy my visits to the salon. It seemed to give me a kind of importance I hadn't experienced before. I had someone to attend on me – only me. I mean, let's face it, for years I've done all the attending – on Jim, at any rate.

As on the previous visit, I came away from the salon feeling very satisfied with my improved appearance, albeit a bit depleted in my finances! It's quite true what they say: you get what you pay for and pay for what you get! Those salon girls are so clever the way they can style hair. I'm sure I'll never be able to do it myself. I paid at the desk on the way out of the salon – no change out of a £10 note! Well, I did give £2 in for a tip as I got a bit flustered! Mrs Jackson once told me it was usual to give a substantial tip at the hairdresser's. Well, my tip was about four times bigger than I had meant to give! I won't be doing that again!

As I walked towards the bus stop I toyed with the idea of treating myself to lunch in the newly opened restaurant in the Town Hall Square, but the sky was beginning to look dark and threatening. I thought could be in for a real downpour, so I decided to get back home. I was lucky for no sooner had I reached the bus stop than a number-10 bus came along and I just managed to get the last seat on it, at the back upstairs. The bus was full of football supporters. It seemed our local team was at home to somebody or other this week – not that I ever took much interest in sport. It was the scarves that caught my eye. Still, I suppose the orange and green added a bit of brightness on such a dull day.

My stop came up sooner than I realised, and I only just got up in time to get off. I hurried when I got off the bus – in fact, I ran along the road, down my path and into the house as giant raindrops bombarded me. So I was only just in time – once again! I don't want to ruin my new hairdo just after I've had it done – not that I'll be going anywhere special to show it off.

Jim didn't even notice anything different about me when I went up to check on him. In fact, he hardly spoke. He gave me the most weird look, which quite unnerved me for a moment. On the table near him was a wooden cross about eight inches high. He'd evidently been carving it. There were bits of wood shavings all round his feet. Perhaps he was turning religious; but then, you can never be sure what Jim has in his mind. As I was about to leave the room, Jim picked up the cross, held it high, pointed it in my direction and made a strange hissing sound, slavering as of old as he did so. It may have been my imagination – I don't know – but all of a sudden I felt an evil presence all around me!

"For God's sake, Martha," I told myself, "pull yourself together. What's got into you?"

Maybe Jim's right: I should get my own mind seen to. That's what Jim told me the other day. He said problems were in my head, not his! I sat down at the kitchen table, my head resting on my folded arms. I tried to make my mind a blank and closed my eyes.

***

It was after two when I awoke. I must have dozed off – it must have happened very quickly. I've never fallen suddenly to sleep like that before in the daytime. I became aware of a pain down one side of my neck. I must have lain awkwardly, and now I am paying for it. I roused myself, went to the bathroom and doused my face with cold water. That woke me up somewhat. Jim had had nothing to eat. I set about making a meal.

***

The rest of the week went by with little of note happening. I wasn't even bothered by a visit from Mrs Jackson. I can't help noticing that she's been going out a lot more of late, and on a regular basis too – nearly every day for the past week. I've seen her come out of the house and she's got into a car with a dark-haired, middle-aged gentleman, and they've driven off at speed. I've not noticed what time she returns home, but return she certainly does for her house has been lit up in the evenings. Maybe she's got herself a 'young man' after all these years. No one seems to know what became of the old one!

Clive has been busy decorating – his lounge, to be precise. I was over there on Sunday evening. He worked hard on the room from early morning, and I knew perfectly well he wouldn't have bothered making himself a meal, so I took him something over. I took him soup, which I reheated on his cooker, and some crusty rolls. He was very glad of it, he said, and he downed it all wolfishly. I'd made some beef sandwiches too, out of leftovers from our joint. That meat was so tender it melted in our mouths. I changed my butcher earlier in the year, and the change has proved a good one indeed, for all the meat I've had from the new man has been excellent, both in taste and in quality. Not that Jim and I are great meat-eaters, but what we do have we enjoy. At least I enjoyed it, and I think Jim did, as far as I can tell anything for sure about Jim these days.

"Don't do any more work tonight, Clive. You look quite worn out," I said.

"I was hoping to finish this wall, but now I've stopped, Martha, I don't feel like carrying on; so I'll take your advice and knock off until tomorrow. I'd much rather sit and talk to you, my love. How about a fresh pot of tea?"

"Good idea! I'll go and make it now," I told him.

Five minutes later saw us chatting happily about this and that, and into a second cup of tea.

"Have you made your mind up yet, Martha, about going to your sister's wedding?" Clive asked.

"I'd certainly like to go, but it's Jim – he's been acting so strange lately I'm not sure what to do. I know you offered to step in and 'mind' Jim, Clive, if I do decide to go. . . . We'll see."

"I was just thinking, Martha, it might help if I come over to see Jim again once or twice so he gets used to me."

"Maybe, Clive. You are still the only person, apart from me, that Jim has ever expressed even the remotest desire to see these past ten years. I'll have a chat with Jim tomorrow and see how the land lies. Let's hope he's in a more co-operative mood than he's been in of late and we might get somewhere. Good heavens, Clive! I've just remembered I've left the oven on; it should have been turned off an hour ago! Must go! See you tomorrow!"

I rushed out of Clive's so fast he had no time to argue the matter. I could smell the casserole as I opened the front door. I'd made the casserole for tomorrow's lunch. It had been in the oven hours. A haze of steam hit me as I opened the oven door. I turned off the gas. When the mist cleared I could see that the casserole was well and truly done – rather too much for my liking, but it was still edible, just about. I added a little water and replaced the lid.

"Just in time again," I thought.

***

Next day I chose my time with care to talk to Jim about Clive coming over to see him.

"At last! At last! Oh, Maggie, you're a good girl," laughed Jim. "I thought he was dead. He was dead, you know, but he's resurrected, has he? Well, that's good news, that is – that's very good news, Maggie." And he roared with laughter again.

So I am Maggie again, am I?

"Yes, Maggie, I want to see Clive. Let him come here when he wants – before that Martha gets back. She won't let anybody in to see me, you know, but Maggie will. She's all right."

***

"Maggie, Maggie, are you there? I want to tell you something. Be quick!" It was Jim calling me back just as I was halfway downstairs.

I turned round and hurried back to him.

"Yes, Jim, what is it you want?"

"Listen – I've got an idea: why don't we have a party, eh? Now, what do you say to that, Maggie?"

Jim was so excited. I hadn't seen him like that for a long time. Even in our courting days he never went over the top, as you might say.

"I don't know about a party, Jim. Who would be there? You have to invite a few people."

"That's no problem, Maggie. There'll be you and me and Clive – not that Martha, mind you; we don't want her coming," Jim said. "I won't have her here at a party – never, no, never!" Jim seemed to be thinking to himself and muttering under his breath. Then he said, "Wait a bit – yes, I've changed my mind. I will have that Martha at the party. Yes, I'll need her there or there won't be any big surprise, will there?" And at the thought of what he said he laughed so much that tears ran down his face.

"I'll see she comes, then, Jim. Leave it to me. But when shall we have this party, Jim?"

"On the 10th, of course. You haven't forgotten the number ten, have you, Maggie? It's special – very special. Always has been," Jim said.

"Well, it's the 11th today, Jim, so you've just missed the 10th. You'll have to wait a whole month now before the 10th comes round again, won't you?"

"It makes no odds. The next one will do just as well. Maybe it'll be better then. Yes, Maggie, I do believe it will."

"And you know what, Jim: it will give me more time to plan our party properly, won't it?"

He failed to answer me, for by this time Jim appeared to have lost all interest in what we'd been discussing. He began to look morose again, and just sat staring in front of him. I'd always found it best to leave him to his own thoughts at such times, so I did just that and went downstairs. It won't surprise me one little bit if he forgets all about the party idea by tomorrow. He is like that. He's done it so many times since his 'illness' I've got used to it. You can never rely on Jim to follow through with anything he's started except maybe his coffin making. A second thought has struck me as I ponder on what Jim said, and it is this: it will be just as well if Jim forgets about his party idea if he is expecting both Maggie and Martha to be in attendance at the same time. I mean, that really would take some doing!

Chapter 43

That evening I went to Clive's. He's almost finished his decorating and very smart it is looking too. He must have worked extremely hard to have got so much done.

"Clive, aren't you clever? It looks lovely. I'd no idea you had such talents. It looks really professional."

"Yes, I'm quite pleased with the results myself, and when everything's back in place it should look good. I felt I had to change this room. It might help me to forget to some extent what happened here," Clive said.

"Maybe it will, Clive, but I think we both know nothing can ever blot out the memory of that awful happening here entirely. Sometimes I think it's a harder punishment to bear not being found out, and it's a life sentence! Oh, I'm sorry, Clive – I shouldn't have said that. I didn't mean to . . ."

I stopped short, then Clive spoke: "It's all right, Martha. You're quite right: nothing will really rid us of those dreadful memories."

He looked round the room and said, "At least it's looking cleaner and brighter in here. But I've some news for you, my dear Martha. Sit down and I'll explain."

All the furniture was heaped up in the middle of the floor covered in dust sheets, and Clive was about to uncover chairs to sit on.

"No, Clive, don't bother about chairs. I'm OK sitting on the carpet."

I settled comfortably enough – in fact we both did – in front of the gas fire.

"I'm curious, Clive: what's this news you have for me, then?"

"Well, Martha, I'm starting work – a job!"

"Good Lord, Clive! You do spring surprises. You starting work – where?"

"You don't need to sound so surprised. I am capable of having a job, you know."

Clive sounded a little bit hurt, I thought.

"Of course you are, Clive. I wasn't implying you weren't. It's just that it's a bit sudden, isn't it? You haven't spoken about getting a job before to me."

"No, I haven't, Martha, though I've been thinking about looking for work for some time – well, since I've been on my own, anyway. Obviously I couldn't hold down a job with Esther as she was.

It was a full-time job looking after her, as you know. Now there's no reason why I shouldn't go to work, is there? And that's exactly what I plan to do. I start next Monday at Sellick's," Clive announced proudly.

"You mean Sellick's, the posh department store in Natesby?" I asked.

"You've got it in one, my dear."

"But, Clive, that's a good ten or twelve miles from here. Think of the travelling," I said.

"You're forgetting, Martha, I have my own transport now, so that won't be a problem, will it?"

"Of course, Clive – I wasn't thinking. But you haven't told me what the job entails. What is it? I'm dying to know."

"Store detective."

"What? However did you land that one?"

"Simple: I went for the interview last Thursday and they rang me today to say I've got the job if I want it and I can start almost immediately. Before I married Esther I had a good job – a security job in London at a large jeweller's – and I've kept references from there when I left. Although they are from years back, they must have done the trick. I do need an income, Martha, and the pay is quite favourable; so what do you think about that?"

"Delighted for you, Clive – absolutely delighted," I said.

I gave him a great hug and a kiss to confirm it.

"But, Clive, why didn't you tell me before that you were going for the interview?"

"Because I wanted to be certain I'd got the job before I said anything. It seems that jobs are not so easy to come by these days, so I consider myself very lucky to have been successful at the first attempt!"

"You're making me feel quite jealous, Clive. I often wish I had a proper job. I had one once, of course, but since Jim . . . Well, you know how it is. It's funny how we've both got so much in common."

"You mean I haven't been able to go to work because of Esther and you are in the same position because of Jim? Yes, you're so right there, Martha – we do both have quite a lot in common. Perhaps that's what attracted us to one another in the first place. Who knows?"

"Martha, I've never discussed my financial affairs with you, but I just want you to know that I'm not exactly on the poverty line."

"Please, Clive, you've no need to explain your affairs to me. I've no wish to pry."

"Pry? What do you mean *pry*? As far as I'm concerned, anything I now have is yours if you need it. Don't you understand? I want you to know how you stand with me in every way. I could manage well enough if I never go to work again. I have several investments which are doing very nicely, thank you. But there are other reasons for wanting to go to work. I need to get some self-confidence back and self-respect. Do you understand, Martha, what I am trying to say?"

"Of course I understand, Clive. I'm glad you're starting a job – I really am. But tell me, Clive: before you married Esther, what exactly did the job involve which you did then?"

"Well, apart from my former security job I was originally trained as a diamond cutter, and I got very well paid for it too."

"But why the security job at the jeweller's, Clive? Why did you change to that?"

"That's rather a long story, Martha, and one which I don't care to recall too often, but I'll tell you. Some diamonds went missing and several of us working in that area were suspected. I was framed by a so-called friend, and although there was insufficient evidence I was sacked anyway. I was so upset at the time I walked out there and then. After that, somehow I got a job in another jewellery firm as a security officer. Quite ironic when you think about it, isn't it?"

"That was rotten luck, Clive, losing your good job like that. Some 'friend' you had, I must say!"

"You live and learn, as they say. Apart from my new job, Martha, I just wanted you to know I've got a few bob anyway – enough to help us on our way when all our present problems are solved."

"Seeing it appears to be confession time, Clive, I'd better tell you how I am situated, then. I may not be quite so well off as you seem to be, but we manage comfortably enough. I had quite a lot of money at one time – mostly from a handsome legacy left to me by one of my father's parishioners, but it's dwindling gradually. It's mostly gone on account of Jim. It's the money I've paid regularly to those doctors who helped 'save' Jim. In a way it's a sort of blackmail, I suppose; but then, where would I be without their help? I'd never have been able to 'save' Jim from the mental home on my own. I've thought a lot lately about what I started over ten years ago and maybe it's all been a sad mistake – I'm not sure!"

"No, Martha, you acted in all good faith over Jim, I'm sure. You've shown great compassion towards him all these years. Surely he must be happier for that."

"Perhaps," I said. "Perhaps. You know, Clive, I've often wondered what would happen to me if I am found out – about Jim's fake funeral and so on. I could end up in prison, as could those doctors who helped me. It's quite frightening, and I don't like to think of it too much."

"Just how much have you been paying those doctors all these years, Martha? I know it's none of my business to ask, and you needn't tell me if you don't want to, only it seems to have been going on so long I'm not surprised your money's going down."

"Yes, Clive, over ten years now I've been paying out. When Jim's needed medication they've supplied it – don't ask me how. Well, I couldn't get it myself, could I? Not with Jim not existing, apparently! In the beginning I sent the doctors a lump sum – a sort of deposit to start the ball rolling. I felt so desperate at the time that I'd have given anybody anything they asked for if only they said they'd help me about Jim. I was in such a state. After all, I was about to marry him! I remember thinking my world had fallen apart at the time, and I just couldn't bear to think of Jim being shut away in a mental institution for the rest of his life. I suppose you could say he's ended up being shut away all these years anyway, but that's the way he's wanted it. It was his choice. He took himself up to that room of his almost as soon as we moved in here, and he's stayed there – apart from his 'work' in the spare room, of course!"

"You mean his coffin making, Martha?"

"Yes, that's right. You didn't see what was in the spare room, did you, Clive? I'll show you Jim's handiwork when you come to see him next time. It makes me wonder just what does go on in Jim's mind, but it seems to please him. After all, Jim was once a master carpenter when he had all his faculties so he still remembers how to do his woodwork. Jim has many peculiar ways which you wouldn't believe, Clive – like he's never expressed a desire to go out and he just stays upstairs. He's never wanted to see anybody but me all these years. Do you realise, Clive, you're the only other human being he's spoken to in over ten years – well, as far as I know, that is. I've never known Jim to venture downstairs – says his legs won't let him. Whatever it is he thinks affects him so keeps him permanently in his room up there."

"Well, you cope with it all marvellously, Martha," Clive said.

"Well, I try. But a while ago you were asking me how much I'd paid these doctors who were helping me, weren't you?"

"Yes, you spoke of a down payment."

"It was £6,000, all in cash."

"Good God, Martha, that was a hell of a lot!" Clive said. He looked visibly shocked.

"I know. I've thought about it since, but at the time I'd have given all I possessed to keep Jim with me. I was assured it was a very risky business, both for the doctors and for me. They forged all sorts of documents on Jim's behalf. Everyone believes Jim is truly dead and buried – except my sister, Ruth, that is. She is the only one in on my dreadful secret. In order to keep up the charade the doctors and I had started, I send them money every quarter and in return they send me any medication Jim might need from time to time. I send the money to a box number, as instructed; and so long as I continue, things seem safe enough as regards what I arranged for Jim so long ago."

"You astonish me, Martha. What risks you have taken! I don't know what to say. All this has cost you so much money and continues to do so. There certainly would be serious repercussions if any of this comes to light. As for those doctors, well, you may think they did you a great favour but they were betraying their calling all right."

"I know that, Clive, but when you're desperate you do desperate things."

"That's true," Clive said, "but we'd never have had the problem of Jim if you'd let the law take its course in the first place, Martha."

I felt angry for the moment at what Clive had just said. He'd never really criticised me before and I didn't like it.

I responded accordingly: "There'd still be the problem of Esther, Clive, or are you forgetting so soon?"

Clive looked at the floor and said nothing. I stood up.

"I'm going, Clive. I've things to do."

And I hurried out of the house, ignoring his attempt at an apology, for he knew he'd upset me. I thought later on that if the law had taken its course regarding Jim, as Clive had suggested, we would never have come to know one another so intimately. It is most unlikely I'd have moved from my own home to live where I am now – opposite Clive's house. I'd never have known he existed! Although I had angry feelings towards Clive for the first time ever, my need of his companionship outweighs the anger. I can't imagine Clive out of my life now, that is for certain!

Chapter 44

Early next morning I had another visit from the Pest Control people. They came on two counts: first to check that we were vermin-free, and secondly to tell me of their findings as regards the remains of the tin of rat poison that I'd used and passed to them for analysis. It seems it was a poison in powder form that an ordinary member of the public should never have had access to. They checked at Hardwick's (the shop I'd bought it from). They found two similar-looking tins the store on sale to the public. They'd taken them to analyse and found that although the tin I'd bought looked exactly the same as the ones he took from Hardwick's, the contents were very different, mine being the odd one out! Hardwick's could not explain how this had come about. The Pest Control people were referred to the suppliers, but even there they drew a blank! So it all remained a mystery still. As for me, I could shed no further light on the matter either. The man left and thanked me for my co-operation, such as it was, saying they'd inform me if, and when, they do come up with an answer. They'd only just nicely gone when Mrs Jackson came over, knocking and entering by the back door at the same time.

"Yes, dear, isn't it just too, too thrilling? Oh my! I don't know if I'm on my head or my heels! I wanted you to be one of the first to know. Now, what do you think of that?" she asked.

Well, quite honestly I don't know what to think. Mrs Jackson getting MARRIED! I had seen her, as I said, going out every day, same time, being picked up by this fellow in a smart suit and being driven away in a smart car. So that must have been the prelude to what she was telling me now. To say I am surprised would be an understatement, but you never can tell about people, can you? I mean, look at Clive and me.

"Come on, dear – you must have something to say about my good news, surely?"

"It's such a surprise, Mrs Jackson, but a pleasant one, I'm sure. I'm only just taking it all in. I'd like to wish you both all the happiness in the world. I really mean that," I told her.

"Yes, I knew you'd be pleased, dear. I can hardly believe it myself, you know, but it's going to happen all right. Oh yes, there's no doubt about that!"

I can't recall Mrs Jackson ever looking so animated. She was happy all right. Well, good luck to her – that's what I say – and long may it last.

"So you'll come to the wedding, won't you, dear? It's on the 10th of next month, a Saturday, by special licence," she said.

I was about to answer her when the thought occurred to me that the 10th is to be the date of my own sister's wedding and Jim's 'party', if it ever comes to be! What a coincidence!

"Is there a problem? You can come, can't you, dear?"

"Well, I'd dearly love to come to your wedding, Mrs Jackson, but it just so happens, by the strangest of coincidences, that I've got an invitation to a wedding already on that very day – my sister is getting married on the same day as you," I told her.

"Good gracious! Imagine that! Well, what a surprise, dear. I don't think I've ever met your sister, have I? I've heard you mention her, though. Well, of course, obviously you must go to your sister's wedding. But I'll tell you what, dear: I wouldn't like to think you can't join in with our happiness at least in some small way, so you must come to the little party we're having a couple of days before the wedding. It'll be at the Havelock Hotel in Natesby from 7 p.m. onwards. It's just for relatives really, and a few special friends, but you must come too, dear. After all, I think I can count you as a special friend too, can't I? You've always been here, a willing listener, whenever I've been in distress, whenever I've needed someone to talk to. Don't think I don't appreciate it, because I do, dear. I don't know what I'd have done sometimes without you to listen to my troubles. There's no one else round these parts I'm willing to confide in. Oh no, they're all far too nosey – always minding somebody else's business! No, dear, you must come at least to our little party before the wedding; so you will come, won't you, dear?" she asked.

"Thank you, Mrs Jackson. Yes, I'll try to be there, but I'm not at all sure I'll even be able to get to my sister Ruth's wedding! It's Jim, you understand, but I'll see what can be done."

"Well, I must admit you are very handicapped there, but sometimes, dear, you have to put what you want first, difficult as it may be! I was just thinking I'll ask Clive next door to my prenuptial celebration. Poor chap, he never seems to go anywhere. Though I don't know if he'll come, I think he will if you come with him; and he has transport now, hasn't he? Have you noticed? Yes, of course you have. How silly of me! Didn't I see you getting into his new car the other week? You know, dear, I think that man has a soft spot for you – I really do! Must go. Lots to do. Bye, dear, for now. I'll tell you more details later on."

And she was gone.

I've always thought that Mrs Jackson looks the picture of health, but this morning she was more than that – she positively glowed! I expect the excitement of her new-found romance and forthcoming marriage account for that. It's funny how I always address her as Mrs Jackson – quite formal, don't you think? But she's always accepted it and never asked me to call her by her Christian name, which I believe is Phyllis. And she never calls me Martha – just 'my dear'. You can't really tell how old Mrs Jackson is. I've always regarded her as about twelve years older than me. It is the reason I always refer to her as 'Mrs Jackson', I suppose – a sort of respect for my elders. My father instilled that into us as children.

I wonder who the lucky chap is she's marrying. She didn't say too much about him, did she? This affair seems to have developed very quickly, which reminds me I'll have to be thinking about my sister's wedding soon and tell her I won't be able to attend, sorry as I am. My sister says her wedding will be a quiet affair – just the bride and groom and me and a few friends, Ruth told me.

As I've told you before, when it was Jim's 'funeral' there were only a couple of relatives in attendance, which proved to be a great advantage as things turned out.

Chapter 45

I still haven't got over my feeling of anger towards Clive at what he said last night. It was probably me being rather petty, I suppose. They do say the course of true love never runs smooth! I'd best forget it, I think.

Oh no! That's Jim knocking on the floor upstairs – summoning my presence, I believe. The knocking is extra-loud and impatient this morning, which means Jim is definitely not in a good mood. Oh well, into battle!

"All right, Jim, no need to knock the floor through. What's wrong?"

"It's dinner time and I've had nothing to eat or drink since yesterday, that's what's wrong!" he bellowed.

"Hang on in there one moment, Jim. First of all, it is not dinner time. It is 10.30 in the morning and I did bring you a cup of tea and some toast earlier, which must be cold now as I see you haven't even touched it. I'll go and make you something now, shall I, seeing that you're starving?" I said rather sarcastically.

He didn't answer.

I picked up his tea and toast and went downstairs to the kitchen. I made Jim poached eggs on toast and fresh tea and went upstairs again.

You'd never have thought there'd been any grumbling from Jim only a little while ago, for he turned to me and smiled and said, "Oh, thank you, Martha. You are good to me. What a lovely breakfast! I'll enjoy this."

I put the tray on the table beside him without saying a word and returned to the sanity of the kitchen. Talk about changeable! That was Jim all right.

I've been looking in my wardrobe today. Just wondered if I could find anything suitable for Mrs J's prenuptial party –that's if I can possibly get there with the problem of Jim. I do have a linen-look outfit I've never worn. I bought it last spring in the sales. I suppose I could get a new hat to go with it. Maybe when I go to town later in the week I'll see something I fancy. I don't think I'll be meeting up with Clive for our pub lunches any more – not now he's working. I'll miss all that.

I've been thinking over the business of Esther's death and the break-in at Clive's. Everything seems to have died down now. It's a welcome lull in that direction. We haven't had any visits from the police now for some time, so that's hopeful. Perhaps Clive and I can get on with our plans for a future together. On the whole it would be best if we both move to another area – some place where nobody knows either of us or anything about us. I will still get help from my doctor friends up north as regards Jim's medication needs and so on. So long as I send regular cheques, all seems well. If we move, Clive and I, Jim will have to live with us anyway, and I wonder how he'd take to that!

"Martha, Martha, have you gone deaf or something?"

It was Jim. I hurried up to him.

"What's all the shouting about, then?" I asked.

"The party, the party. When is it, then, eh? Have you got it all fixed up, eh?" Jim asked excitedly.

"Oh, that. No, it's not arranged yet, Jim, but there's plenty of time so don't be worrying yourself about it."

"I want it soon, do you hear? I want Clive there. He must be there for certain. And I want Maggie there as well, and my sister can come if she likes. Don't forget her, will you?" Jim threw his head back and gave a great guffaw. He really seemed to be enjoying thoughts of a party.

I expect Jim meant *my* sister when he said *his* sister. Well, he hasn't got one, has he? It's just as well I understand him. Nobody else would. Oh, and I am Maggie again, am I? Jim wants Maggie at his party – that'll be fun. I'll have to cut myself in two, won't I? One half Martha and the other Maggie. It'll be interesting to see how that works out!

For the past few days Jim's been occupied with his 'brew', as he calls it. He started sometime ago making a kind of wine. At least, I think that's what he's been concocting. He asked me to get him empty wine bottles, and I see he's filled about six so far. I had to get him various fruits, some spirits and concentrated lemon and lime. He's asked for molasses sugar too. I never heard of winemakers putting that in the mix, but maybe it is used. I wouldn't know. I'm not very knowledgeable on such matters. It's keeping Jim happy, at any rate. He says he's made all this for the party. It will surely be the oddest party there has ever been!

Chapter 46

"Are you there, dear? It's only me. I've brought you something. Go on, dear – try it on."

It was Mrs Jackson, and she handed me a large carrier bag.

"What is it?" I asked.

"Have a look. Take it out of the bag," she said.

I did as I was bid. Out of it came the most beautiful pale-green coat-dress I think I've ever seen, cut on classical lines in heavy silk. The green shaded from palest eau de Nil to mid-apple at the hem. You could tell it was expensive – a one-off original, I should imagine. Mrs Jackson didn't buy anything that wasn't expensive. She has good taste, I'll give her that. She evidently has the money to back it up too, which must always be a help. I held the garment up to see the full effect of the style and shading.

"Oh, it's absolutely beautiful – so elegant too. Is this to be your going-away outfit, then?" I asked.

"No, dear, don't be silly. It's not for me; it's for you, dear. I was sure it would fit you. I've put a bit too much weight on to wear it any more. Mind you, I only wore it once myself. It's as new, as they say in the Bargain Basement, eh? You said the other day you were wondering what on earth to wear to your sister's wedding, and yesterday I was having a clear-out of my wardrobe and I found this little number. I thought to myself, 'Why, that's the very thing for Martha to wear at her sister's wedding – that's if you can ever get there, what with the problem of Jim. But it's all yours, dear, if you'd like it; and I'll be only too happy if you'll keep it," she told me.

"I don't know what to say. It's so elegant."

"Look, Martha – try it on. Go on."

I slipped my skirt and blouse off gingerly and put the green outfit on. It fitted perfectly. You'd think it had been made for me. I looked at myself in the hall mirror and I had to admit it looked a million dollars!

"My, but it's even better than I thought it would be on you, dear, and it does wonders for your figure and no mistake. You simply must keep it. It really suits you."

"Mrs Jackson, I can't just take this. You must let me pay you something for it – I insist," I said.

"I wouldn't hear of it, dear. I'm only too pleased for you to have it. I've got some other stuff you might like too – some that won't fit me any more – and it's practically new. If you don't have it I'd only throw it away or, at best, send it to a jumble sale. Come on over sometime and pick out anything you think might be useful to you. I must go, dear – I'm meeting Harry in ten minutes. Bye."

And she was off like the wind.

So that was the lucky man's name: Harry. I put the coat-dress on a hanger I had to hand and took it upstairs to my wardrobe. I smoothed it into place. Yes, that will do very nicely for my sister's wedding – very nicely indeed. Except it is unlikely I'll be able to get there.

On reflecting on Mrs Jackson's visit, I recalled that during the meeting she had addressed me just the once by my name – Martha – instead of her usual 'my dear'. Well, that was a first.

***

"Oo-ooh! Me again! Are you there, dear?"

I hurried downstairs. Mrs Jackson was calling through the front-room window, which was open.

"Yes, here I am. I've just been hanging the dress-coat you gave me up in my wardrobe. I don't know how to thank you. I'm so thrilled with it, I can tell you."

"Oh, say no more. You're most welcome, as I said before. I'll tell you what I've come back for: could you keep an eye on my house for the next few days, dear? I'm going away with Harry to meet his brother and sister

176

and some friends of his in Oxford. I think they must want to give me the once-over or something. You don't mind, do you, dear?"

"Of course not. Don't worry – I'll keep a lookout. You just go off and I hope you enjoy it."

"Thanks, dear. I'm sure I will. I never ever imagined myself marrying again! Oh, and there might be a parcel coming for me. Would you keep it for me, dear? I'll leave a note at my house for it to be delivered to you," she said.

And away she pranced like a two-year-old. 'It's wonderful what love can do for you,' I thought. Wouldn't it be nice if Clive and I can do the same? But then, our circumstances are not quite so easy.

My sister rang this morning to confirm arrangements for her wedding – times, venues and so on. I hadn't the heart just yet to tell Ruth that I won't be able to get to her wedding, but I'll have to tell her in the end, I know. Evidently my sister is getting married at a registry office. I'm sure our father would never have approved of that. He firmly believed that christenings, marriages, funeral services and the like should all be conducted in the right place – namely, in a church. Still, he's been long gone now, as has my mother, and times change, as they say. I wonder what my father would think of us today about this and that. Funny, but I don't seem to think of my mother half so much.

My mother was a good soul – the old-fashioned type of wife, compared with nowadays, that is. She was subservient, thinking a wife's place was in the home. She believed my father could do no wrong – his word was law and all that. But then, they did in those days, didn't they? That's just how it was. We were very strictly brought up in every way. I expect my parents would consider me quite wayward now by their standards, what with my relationship with Clive and so on. And as for what I did to help Clive when Esther died, well, they'd never handle that one! I don't know what they'd say about Jim.

There was a rattle at the letter box. More junk mail, I supposed. I went to investigate. Hm! Would you believe it? Three envelopes here. I'm lucky if I get three in a week usually. I looked to see if any of them were of interest. Not the first two, anyway. But what was this? I opened it. Just listen, will you? Good Lord, I don't believe it! I hardly ever fill in a pools coupon, but I did one last week – I don't know why. I've had a small win, it seems – my first ever! Not a fortune, but most acceptable: £642! What a lovely surprise! I must have been inspired last week. I never bother to check my pools coupon usually, but I'm so pleased. I'll buy my sister something nice with some of this money, and I'll get some extras for Jim's party – that's if Jim hasn't forgotten he ever asked for a party.

I wonder how Clive will like his new job. I saw him going off early this morning. He'd left his bedroom light on. Obviously he's not used to his new routine yet. I'll go over this evening and he'll be able to tell me how his first day went. I'll cook him something as a surprise. I don't suppose he's planned ahead much yet. He's not been very organised with his meals since Esther died. When she was alive he had to maintain regular mealtimes for her sake, but he tends to neglect himself somewhat now. He'll have to do better now he's working.

It'll be good for him to mix in fresh company at work. I think he's missed out a lot on male company all these years, and it shows in some ways. I noticed it most when his brother came to visit. Clive seemed almost ill at ease with him. Talk about chalk and cheese!

Chapter 47

I quite enjoyed myself this afternoon going round the shops. I put my winnings cheque in the bank and also drew out some money. My current account hasn't as much in it as I thought. I really should take more notice of my monthly bank statements. Still, there are always my stocks and shares to fall back on if I should need extra. I would never have owned such things if I hadn't had that large legacy left to me years ago. I was advised to invest most of it, which I did, and the dividends have been very satisfactory so far.

It took me some time to choose a present for my sister's wedding. At first I toyed with the idea of something practical, like crockery or bedding, but I'm sure she's got all she needs of that. Then I saw it in a jeweller's shop window: a cuckoo clock! It might sound silly, but I decided on that. I know my sister has often said she'd like to have a cuckoo clock someday, and I'm sure she never got one. It isn't the kind of thing you'd buy for yourself probably. The common or garden things always claim priority, it would seem. Ruth mentioned over the phone also that when she got settled down with Charlie there were two things she was determined to treat herself to: first a shower for the bathroom, and secondly a birdbath for the garden. That's if she stays living where she is now, in her own house, but maybe she'll be going to live in Charlie's house. She hasn't said yet.

But where was I? Oh yes, outside the jeweller's shop eyeing the cuckoo clock in the window. I had never been in this particular shop before. I'd had little occasion to buy jewellery, anyway. As I went through the door an old bell tinkled above the shop door. I hadn't come across one like that for many years. I went into the shop down two well-worn stone steps. It was an old-fashioned shop, cluttered with all manner of things. There were clocks small, medium and large, grandfather and grandmother clocks; there were trays of rings on velvet in cases – wedding rings, engagement rings, eternity rings, bracelets, wristwatches . . . There was very little trouble taken with making an effective display, it seemed to me. It all seemed to have assembled itself by chance, in great contrast to those affluent-looking jewellers with their deep-pile carpets and sophisticated lighting and decor. I once happened to go in Samuel's with Mrs Jackson when she'd been buying some new earrings, and that was an experience in how the other half lives! This little shop was very different – one of the last of the old-time jewellers, I should think. It wouldn't have been out of place in a Victorian novel.

"Can I help you, madam?" The voice sounded thin and old.

I had to look twice to see where the voice came from. A diminutive old man peered over gold-rimmed spectacles at me from behind a heavy oak counter.

"Oh, er, yes. I was wondering how much the cuckoo clock in the window is, please?"

He did not answer, but turned and pulled aside the faded green velvet curtain which acted as a backdrop to the window display. He stood on the second step of a small pair of steps to reach the cuckoo clock. I feared he might topple backwards as he stepped down, for he and the stepladder appeared very unsteady. He paused a moment to regain his balance and turned to me, clock in hand.

"There you are," he said, putting the clock down carefully on the counter.

I could see a ticket tied to the metal ring at the back of the clock. It showed the price of £38.

"Beautiful clock, madam – a work of art, you might say. Lovely wood, hand-carved, and it's £38 as you can see from the ticket. Swiss, of course."

He handed the clock to me for closer inspection. It did indeed seem an attractive buy.

"Yes, it is a very nice-looking clock. It's for a wedding present, you see. Yes, I'll take it. It does have a guarantee, doesn't it?" I asked.

"Naturally, madam. Three years, but I wouldn't be surprised if it goes on for a lifetime. The Swiss make such great clocks and watches. This cuckoo clock is the last of its kind, I'm afraid, and I don't expect to get further supplies, unfortunately," he told me. "Gift-wrapped, madam? I can do that for you."

"That would be very helpful," I said.

"Before I wrap it, you'll want to hear the cuckoo, I should think, and it's just on the hour now."

"Cuckoo, cuckoo, cuckoo."

And three times the bird popped out of its little house. It was so cute.

"Oh, that's just great," I told the jeweller.

I watched as the old man lovingly wrapped up the clock. I paid for the clock, thanked him and left the shop feeling well pleased with my purchase.

Next I bought a few bits for Jim's party and a pair of shoes to go with the outfit Mrs Jackson had given me.

I'd just missed the bus home, so slipped into a café Clive and I had used on several occasions. I had a pot of tea for one and a scone. I dawdled there until it was time for the next bus. I had to run for it when I left the café, and caught it by the skin of my teeth. When I got my breath back I realised why I'd nearly missed the bus: my watch had stopped ten minutes beforehand. Ten? That struck a chord somewhere inside. It was a long time since I'd thought about the occurrence of that number in my life. Coincidence, I guess.

When I got home I examined my purchases and checked my expenditure. Good Lord! Only £18 left out of the £100 – I have spent more on the shoes than I intended.

I made a cup of tea and took one up to Jim. I was surprised to find him still in bed!

"You all right, Jim?" I asked.

He didn't answer at first, then he said, "Why are you keeping me in bed?"

"What on earth are you talking about, Jim? I'm not keeping you in anywhere. You can get up or stay in bed just as you please, and well you know it. Here – I've brought you a cup of tea."

I put the tea on his bedside locker, but Jim made no move and continued to stare at the ceiling.

"Jim, you're not ill, are you?" I asked.

For answer he turned to look at me and started one of his maniacal laughs. It got louder as it gathered momentum, and then he became silent suddenly, like someone had switched him off. I left him and went downstairs. I didn't even bother to tell him I'd bought stuff for his party. He'd probably never speak about it again, anyway; but if he did, I was prepared – food-and-drink-wise at least.

Downstairs I had a bit of a rest and read the paper. There seemed to be a bit of banging about coming from upstairs. At least Jim was out of bed now, it seemed. I waited a while then made Jim something to eat. He usually only wanted a cup of tea and a bit of cake at this time of day. I took his eats up on a tray. When I went into his room I saw what all the banging had been about. He'd done some rearranging of his room: he'd moved his bed from one side of the room to the other. It now stood by the window. His bedside locker was in the middle of the room and he'd placed the two armchairs side by side; they'd always been at opposite ends of the room before.

"Should I leave your tray on the locker, Jim?"

"Well, there's nowhere else to put it, is there?" he rapped in quite a grumpy tone.

"No, I suppose there isn't, but where's your little round table gone, for goodness' sake?"

"Where do you think? It's in the party room, of course, and you'll need to bring some more chairs up for the party," Jim said. Jim was almost shouting as he spoke.

"What do you mean, Jim – the party room? I didn't know we had one of those!"

"Next door, next door. God, woman, you're getting worse and that's a fact!"

He meant the spare room, of course. So we were having the party in there, were we? Along with the coffins! Nice!

"I'm pleased you haven't forgotten about the party, then, Jim. Still on, is it?"

"Of course it's still on, and I hope you've prepared what's got to be done. I want this to be a party to remember, though I might be the only one to remember anything! Ha ha ha ha! You'll see, you'll see." He cackled away for quite a time at whatever it was that amused him so.

"What makes you think you'll be the only one to remember anything, then, Jim? Do you think we'll all be so drunk we won't know any more till the next day?"

"Ha ha ha! That won't be far from the truth either," Jim said gleefully, and he continued his mad cackling.

"What I don't understand, Jim, is why you've changed everything round in here. What's it all about, then?"

"I have my reasons, so don't ask," he told me.

He hobbled from his armchair to the locker in the middle of the room and stood there, a sandwich in each hand, eating one and holding on to the other. I noticed he was dragging one leg quite badly as he moved. It could be for show or it could be for real. The possibility of a slight stroke crossed my mind. I didn't remark on it to Jim. I left him to his tea. If he wants to stand up to have his tea, then that is up to him.

Chapter 48

My sister rang this evening. She was as excited as ever about all the arrangements for her wedding. Charlie, it seems, has booked a surprise ten-day honeymoon for them both in Paris in one of the top hotels. It is his wedding gift to Ruth. It seems he lived in France at one time, for over five years, in connection with his job, and he speaks French fluently. My sister has never learned French at school, and neither have I. It wasn't a subject that was taught at the school we attended, funnily enough. We had a bit of Latin and that was our lot as far as languages were concerned.

"Now, you're definitely coming to our wedding, Martha, aren't you? You'll be the only relative I'll have there. Charlie's having a few of his side there, so with you there'll be ten of us. All right, Martha?"

I assured her I'd do my best to be there and wished her well with all her arrangements. I still can't bring myself to tell her I won't be there. I know I'll have to tell her soon.

Paris, eh? I don't suppose I'll ever go there myself, but good luck to Ruth – and Charlie, of course! How many did she say there'd be at the wedding? Ten? Yes, she did say ten – another ten in our lives, it seems! Well, no, it'll be nine without me.

Chapter 49

Clive was full of his first day at work when I went over to see him. I noticed he'd only been home about twenty minutes. I'd seen him arrive.

"Well, how did your first day go?" I asked.

"I think it went very well, though I do say so myself. It's a big store all right, but it seems a happy place to work in. I was attached to a Mr Van Clark. I shadowed him all day. I'll be with him for the first week, they told me – showing me the ropes, so to speak. It seems he's been with the firm for over twelve years. I'll learn a lot from him, I can see. There's more to this job than meets the eye, you know, Martha. For one thing, I've to write a report each day for the office staff, and any difficulties arising will be ironed out in the first hour of the day following. I tell you what: my feet don't half ache! I must have walked a mile or two today already, up and down floors and round the numerous departments. Still, don't think I'm grumbling, because I'm not. It feels great to be going to a job after all these years away from one. Heavens! I'll bet you've never known me talk so much at once, have you? But how's your day been, Martha? You look tired."

"I'm all right. It's lovely to see you so happy and excited, Clive, after your first day at work. I'm so pleased for you."

"Come on, Martha – tell me what you've been up to. I've been talking too much about me already."

"Well, I went to town and bought my sister's wedding present, and I bought some new shoes for the 'big day', and that's about it. The trouble is I know I can't get to my sister's wedding. Also Mrs Jackson has invited me to her pre-wedding party, but I can't go to that either. But never mind. Oh, I didn't tell you, did I? Mrs Jackson came over to tell me she is getting married. Now, isn't that a surprise? She's so excited."

"Good Lord! No, Martha, you didn't tell me. What a surprise!" Clive said. "She's a dark horse, all right. Pity it's not us tying the knot, Martha, my love. But Martha, what's that appetising smell? I noticed you stopped in the kitchen for a minute on your way in here."

"The fact is, Clive, I made you a casserole. I thought you might not have eaten properly today, it being your first day at work."

"That's so sweet of you, Martha. What a pleasant surprise! I won't pretend that it isn't welcome, because it most certainly is. That delicious smell really sets my taste buds working. There is a canteen at work for the staff, but I just had a coffee at lunchtime. I felt a bit anxious, I suppose, on my first day. I didn't fancy a meal then, but, by Jove, I do now, for who could resist a smell like that? You're a great cook, Martha, and you always make a tasty casserole."

"*Always*, Clive? I think you've only had one from me before this, but thanks for the compliment!"

"That's where you're wrong, my love – two. You've made me two," Clive assured me.

"OK, two it is; but, look – go and get this one while it's still hot. It's on 'low' under the grill. I'll leave you to get your meal. Oh, I knew there was something else I had to tell you: you left your bedroom light on this morning when you went to work."

"Did I? I'd better check everything's off tomorrow before I leave, eh? I'll be leaving the cooker or the fire on next. I could come home and find the house burned down!" Clive joked.

"Clive, don't even joke about such things. It isn't funny."

"I'm only pretending, but it could happen, Martha. You're a bit edgy today, Martha. What's wrong?"

"Nothing – well, not really. It's just Jim has been going on about his party. You'll have to come, Clive – he's expecting you."

"Don't worry, Martha – I'll be there all right."

"It'll be a weird affair, I'm sure, but if that's what Jim wants . . . Look, Clive – go and get your meal before it spoils. I've kept you from it for long enough."

"Right – I will. And thanks so much for cooking for me. You are such a darling."

"Of course I am," I said coyly.

I started to leave, but not before Clive pulled me into his arms in a strong embrace. We kissed and parted. As I left I glanced at Mrs Jackson's house. I wondered when she'd be back – a few days, I think she said. It seems strange to see her house in darkness and not a suggestion of a curtain twitching! That proves beyond doubt she is not in residence.

***

I'd only just got up on Friday when the doorbell rang. I answered it and there was yet another parcel for Mrs Jackson – a different name was on the delivery van this time, and the parcel was smaller than the last one, but quite heavy nevertheless. I took it from the van man as he remarked about some notice on Mrs Jackson's door to leave any parcel at number 10 if she is out. I assured him that it was in order and signed for the delivery.

I spent most of the day having a good clean-up in preparation for the party taking place soon. I don't know why I bothered – there isn't going to be anyone much there, is there? Only Jim and me and Clive. Of course Jim had invited that 'Martha' too – said he'd need her there especially. Mind you, that was when he was thinking of me as Maggie. He may have changed again by tomorrow, and he may know me as Martha again, in which case I'll have to explain that Maggie can't make it, if you see what I mean. It's a bit complicated, I have to admit! He might understand and he might not. Whatever it was Jim would be thinking, either way, there could only be one of me there.

By ten o'clock I'd come down with a terrible headache – more of a migraine really – and I decided that if I was to be in any kind of shape to cope with the party and Jim, then I'd best get to bed early for once. I'd need a good night's sleep.

I did just that – after seeing to Jim, of course and his tablets. At least, I would have seen to Jim and his tablets except that for the first time ever that I can remember Jim refused point- blank to take his tablets at all.

"But, Jim, you won't sleep without them," I told him.

He just laughed and put the tablets in the old leather bag he kept money in. I've always seen he has some money – from me, of course. I reckon it gives him a bit of dignity.

I left him and went to bed. As I put my bedroom light off I saw, as I drew back the curtains, that Clive's bedroom light was on and downstairs was in darkness. It looked like he meant to have an early night too. I got into bed, hoping my headache would soon be gone.

***

I woke next morning early, and thank goodness my headache was gone!

I rang my sister and told her I definitely would not be going to her wedding because of Jim. Naturally, she was very upset, but said she understood in the circumstances and she'd explain the reason to Charlie – not the real reason, I knew, but she'd come up with something believable, no doubt. After all, the less said about the true situation the better, and, as far as other people were concerned, Jim had died years ago, hadn't he?

Now for the big battle! The day of the party! I was feeling very uneasy indeed. I couldn't say exactly what caused it. I don't really believe in premonitions, but that morning I felt as near to having one as I've ever done in my life. There was almost an air of evil about the place. Whatever it was, try as I might, it wouldn't leave me. There was definitely an air of impending doom! Coming on a bit strong there, aren't I? But the feeling, whatever it was, well, that was very strong too.

In the midst of my gloomy thoughts I was shocked into reality by a loud banging from upstairs: Jim again. When I got up there he was talking to himself. I thought that was what he was doing, but Jim told me he was talking to Maggie. What do you want, Martha?" he bellowed. "Can't you see I'm talking to Maggie? Getting jealous, are you, eh?" he asked as he cackled away at the thought.

"What do I want, Jim? I thought you needed me here, judging by all that knocking you did on the floor." I thought I'd better humour him, so I said, "I'm sorry – I didn't see Maggie sitting there."

"What do you mean *sitting*? She's standing, isn't she? And why is she standing, eh? Cos you've taken my chairs away. You can be a nasty bitch when you want to, Martha."

"Wait a minute, Jim, I have not taken any chairs anywhere, but I'm not blind. I can see they are no longer in here, so where are they, then?"

"How should I know? Go and find one for Maggie to sit on. She's come all this way to be at my party – to see me, mind, not to see you. No, she's no reason to want to see you – *ever!*" Jim screamed at me.

With that outburst he picked up his stick and started banging on the floor again.

This time he beat out a definite rhythm, which he kept repeating, humming some kind of a tune to it. It was a familiar rhythm, but I couldn't quite place it at first. It came to me later: the rhythm fitted exactly the first few bars of Chopin's Funeral March! Charming, I must say. Jim was fond of all kinds of music – or he had been when he was in his right mind. I remembered that. Perhaps a few rhythms had stayed with him. He had taken to humming a few tunes lately as well, come to think of it. I left him to his knocking and said I'd bring him a cup of tea shortly.

"Two teas, Martha – two. Don't forget Maggie here," he said.

On the way out I saw the spare-room door was open a fraction. I looked in. Yes, sure enough there were the two armchairs, one facing each coffin. I don't know when Jim moved those in there, I'm sure. I am surprised he's had the strength to do all this moving of late. I have the impression he's got so much weaker lately. Still, he appears to have managed it all very well.

In the afternoon I made two quiches, a variety of dainty sandwiches and a selection of small cakes and biscuits. I'd also bought a party-type cake from town, and we'd cut that in due course. Seeing that Jim had been going on so long about wanting a party, I thought I'd better make it look authentic.

At four o'clock I popped over to Clive's and told him to come to the party around seven o'clock. He was busy ironing a shirt when I went in. It looked quite an expensive one.

"New?" I asked.

"Yes, I bought it where I work. I get ten per cent discount there, you know – one of the perks of the job. I could get stuff for you, Martha, if you want anything."

"Hm, could be useful. Thanks, Clive. I might take you up on that one of these days. You don't need to iron that shirt when it's new, Clive!"

"Of course I do. Look at the folds where it's been packed," Clive said.

It was then I caught sight of a new suit draped over the back of the settee.

"Not a new suit as well, Clive?"

"Yes, it is new. It's for Jim's party, my dear. I thought we ought to do the best we can for him and anyway I needed some new clothes. If we make something of the evening, Jim might really enjoy himself."

"If you say so. Anyway, see you around seven, Clive. Don't bring anything – just yourself."

"I won't, then. I look forward to it."

"You might be sorry too!" I said.

Chapter 50

When I got home Jim was ranting and raving upstairs and banging about.

"What's wrong now, Jim? Why all the noise?"

"She's gone! I knew she would. You've got rid of her again, haven't you? You'll pay for this – by God, you will!"

"Listen, Jim – I'll be gone myself one of these days if you don't stop all this rubbish!"

Suddenly I felt extremely angry. Usually I kept my temper very well with Jim, but for some reason today I felt at the end of my tether.

"It isn't rubbish. Tell 'em to stop, Martha. They shouldn't do it – no, they shouldn't be doing that at all. What time is it?"

"It's half past four, Jim, and your party's at seven o' clock."

"There! You see, you've got it wrong again, Martha. Didn't I tell you ten o'clock, eh? Have you forgotten?"

"Ten o'clock, Jim? But that's a bit late to start, isn't it?"

"Not at all, Martha. You see, ten's always been lucky for me," said Jim, laughing away to himself.

"If you say so, Jim. Ten o'clock it will be, then."

And with that, I left him.

So I had to inform Clive of the change of time. He seemed amused by it all. I must say, I wasn't. Something was brewing, I knew!

***

At nine fifty-eight there was a knock on the front door. Usually people ring the bell.

"Come in, Clive. Nice of you to come. My, but you do look smart. You must be going somewhere special," I said sarcastically. I welcomed Clive particularly loudly so Jim would hear what I said.

When we got upstairs Jim was nowhere to be seen; he was not in his room, though I went back in there for a second look. Then we heard it: a kind of whining coming from the spare room, and it gradually got louder. Clive and I went in there just in time to see Jim rise from one of the coffins he'd made, and then he stepped out of it and stood staring.

Jim had changed his clothes. He was all dressed up in his black suit and a black tie. He was wearing black leather gloves too. Oh well, there is no accounting for his strange ways. It was the first time Clive had seen Jim's handiwork, and it was clear he could not hide his astonishment and shock.

"Now, Jim, greet your guest. Here he is – Clive," I said.

"Good, good. Oh, Clive, I'm glad she let you come. Sit down here by me. No, not there – this side. That's Maggie's chair. You haven't met her, have you, Clive? Maggie, this is Clive," Jim said.

Oh, so Maggie was back now, was she? Jim said I'd sent her away, if I remember. Never mind. I could see Clive was looking extremely confused, but he coped very well, I thought, shaking hands and smiling at an imaginary Maggie on the empty chair on Jim's left.

"Lovely, isn't she, Clive?" said Jim.

"Very beautiful indeed," said Clive.

"I knew you'd think so. She's been very good to me – oh yes, very good. That Martha tried to get rid of her, you know, but she didn't manage it. No, Maggie's back with me now," Jim told Clive.

It was a very strange evening. Jim spent most of his time talking to 'Maggie' and listening to whatever it was she was supposed to be saying. Well, it certainly made him laugh – non-stop almost. That's the idea, isn't it? You're supposed to enjoy yourself at a party, aren't you? I don't know what Clive made of it all, I'm sure.

We ate most of what I had prepared and had a few drinks –non-alcoholic, as I didn't want alcohol having a bad effect on Jim. He could be wild enough as it was. The funny thing was that Jim asked particularly for lemon juice so that was what he got.

I had to keep pouring a drink for 'Maggie', as Jim instructed – of course

I went along with it. Not much conversation went on between the three of us – or should that be the four of us? Well, Jim thought there were four of us there – didn't he? – including his Maggie, whom he thought he was talking to. Clive and I were kind of spectators. I'll bet Clive had never been to a party like this one ever in his life!

The time had got to eleven o'clock, and I was thinking "Is this it, then – the party?"

Suddenly Jim stood up.

"Now," he said, "I've got a surprise for you."

He went off to an old cupboard at the end of the room and brought out two bottles. He put one down on the table and took the cork out of the other one. It had no label on it. It looked very much like one of his own concoctions. I was right – it was. He insisted we all have a drink. I remembered the last time Jim had given Clive one of his drinks and Clive had been very ill after it.

"No, thanks, Jim," Clive said. "I really don't want a drink."

"But you haven't had any of this yet, man. This is a new one I've made and there's not another one like it. Here – taste it. Go on!"

And Jim poured some of his mixture into a glass and forced it on Clive.

"Here, Martha, this one's for you. I won't begrudge you a drink."

"What about Maggie?" I couldn't resist asking.

"Maggie? Maggie? She went a long time ago – oh yes, a very long time ago!"

Jim appeared to have tears in his eyes as he spoke. So it was going to be one of those evenings was it? So be it. I saw Jim had poured himself a drink from the other bottle – no label on that one either.

"Drink up, man, drink up," Jim told Clive. "You too, Martha. I took a lot of trouble making this."

"It's a bit strong, Jim," Clive said.

"Rubbish – drink it down, both of you," Jim said.

The slower we appeared to be drinking the more agitated Jim became. He began to get angry and started stamping about. I feared he might even become violent so whispered to Clive that it might be best to do what Jim wanted and drink the lot down. We both did this. The taste was bad. I know Clive thought it was horrible too, judging by the look on his face!

Jim calmed down after this and seemed pleased we'd drunk his concoction down. He even looked in our glasses to make sure it had all gone.

"Good, good. That's good." He went to the cupboard and brought out yet another bottle, opened it and said, "Here – have another drop, both of you. I mean, we want to make sure, don't we, eh?"

And Jim poured a liberal amount for Clive and me.

"Go on – drink it. What are you waiting for? Drink it, damn you!"

I could see Jim was getting extremely agitated again. He had a wild look in his eyes such as I had never seen before. It frightened me. Jim then appeared to lunge out at Clive, but stopped just short. At this, Clive drained his glass, but I managed to empty mine behind me, into a plant pot, while Jim wasn't looking.

Jim began to sing. It wasn't so much a song as a dirge. He kept urging us to join in, which was difficult as we didn't know the tune – if there ever was one, that is. This went on for some time, and it was then that I saw Clive holding his head in his hands. I didn't feel too good myself. It must have been that brew of Jim's. I was certain that was what had made Clive so ill once before.

Jim seemed well enough, but then he'd drunk from a different bottle, hadn't he? Jim stood up and started banging on the table, like he was calling a meeting to order.

"Listen," he said, "do you know what we haven't done yet? We haven't cut the party cake. We must do that. Oh yes, we must do that, all right. Now, where's that knife, Martha? Oh, there it is. Feel that – nice and sharp. See – I gave it a good sharpening-up. We want neat, clean cuts, don't we now? Nothing messy, eh?"

And as if to show how sharp the knife was, Jim sliced through several layers of paper serviettes with one clean cut. Then he gave a kind of skip and hop – well, as good as he could manage now his leg dragged so badly. He kept waving his knife about and laughing. He cut into the cake, levering out three very uneven, jagged pieces, but he didn't hand them round.

Immediately after the cake-cutting, Jim became very excited and agitated again as he said, "Now, Clive, what we need is another drink."

"No, no – no more, please. I don't feel very well. I don't think your brew agrees with me, Jim. I'm afraid I'm going to have to go home," Clive said in a very shaky voice. He tried to stand up to leave, but moved as if his feet were made of lead.

"It's a lie-down you need, Clive, and you shall have one. I've got the very thing for a good rest. Here – let me help you. You can have a rest in my beautiful casket. Come on, Martha – lend a hand, will you?"

Jim's face shone with a kind of wild excitement as he spoke. I don't know why or how, but I found myself with Jim pushing Clive into a coffin – the first one Jim had made.

Clive himself seemed incapable of offering any resistance once 'laid out' there. He simply shut his eyes and breathed heavily. When I looked at his hands I saw his nails were turning blue, as were his lips. I began to panic.

"Jim! Jim, what have you done to Clive? Look at him! We must get a doctor quickly. There's no time to lose!"

Jim just looked at me, waving his knife around and smiling his evil smile as if he was master of the situation. Well, he was the master, for I hardly had the energy to move. What had happened to me?

"That's right, Martha, you go and get a doctor – if you can! You'll never make it!" He laughed out loud at his own remarks.

I knew I had to get help for Clive, and without delay. I was just about to make for the stairs when, to my horror, I found I could barely move. It was almost as if I was becoming paralysed. I began to feel numb all over. The more I struggled, the less I could move. I must have blacked out – for how long, I don't know. When I came to I opened my eyes. All I could see was a blur, but gradually the mist cleared. I still had little feeling in my body. I appeared to be lying down. I was. My God! I was in the other coffin Jim had made! He must have dragged me there when I blacked out. They say with madness great strength can come, even from the normally weakest person. Well, Jim had found it from somewhere. With the shock of where I was, I made an almighty effort and somehow raised myself to a sitting position, leaned my weight to one side and more or less tumbled out of the coffin.

I looked round – no Jim in sight. I dragged myself towards the other coffin. The lid was partly on. With difficulty I slid the lid further off. I must have been too shocked to let out a scream. There was Clive; the knife which Jim had been brandishing stuck out of Clive's chest. Blood was seeping everywhere! There was no movement. Clive was DEAD!

Oh, my God! What was to happen now? I'd found Esther dead and now I'd found Clive dead too! I was numbed in mind and body. I don't know how long I stayed staring – I was in deep shock! I pulled myself nearer to Clive. What a scene of horror! My dear love had been murdered, stabbed to death by a maniac, for that is surely what Jim is, and only he could have done this.

How can I live without Clive? I bent over and kissed his face, his lips, his body, wetting my lips with his blood.

Oh, God, can this be real? It's a nightmare from hell. I was in utter despair. Then my shock turned to anger. The bastard! The wicked bastard! Jim had killed the only thing I loved – the one hope I had of happiness on this earth. Oh, God, my poor darling Clive. Why him? Why? I'd got to get help although it was too late to help Clive.

It was that drink that Jim gave us that started all this. He must have planned it all for months. Mad as Jim is, he had used what wits he has to plan all this. He must have meant me to die too. I only had half as much of Jim's 'brew' as Clive had, and I nearly didn't come through it. In fact, I know I am far from right now. I have an unbearable burning feeling in my stomach.

"Oh, God, please, please help me!" I cried.

I kept blacking out, but after what seemed an age I reached the top of the stairs.

The phone – yes, that's what I knew I must do: call the police, an ambulance, anything. I was about to try to get downstairs when I felt a thud on the back of my head, then another, then another and I began falling, falling! I felt something behind me, falling too, laughing that maniacal laugh.

Jim!

Chapter 51

Two police cars and an ambulance were standing outside 10 Exton Avenue on the morning following Jim's party. A call had been received at the police station from a man telling the police to go to Exton Avenue quickly for he thought something dreadful had happened there! He evidently rang off without giving a name or any further details. The police had gone there immediately and gained entrance by the back door, which had been left open. They found an unconscious woman at the foot of the stairs with a bloodstained knife in her hand. Upstairs they found a man in a coffin, dead, with several stab wounds to his chest. There was a further coffin in the room empty. There did not appear to be anyone else in the house. This was a bizarre case and would take some solving! Fingerprints and photographs were taken and the woman was taken in the ambulance to hospital. She had a serious head wound. It was questionable whether or not she would survive the paramedics declared. Later a second ambulance arrived and removed the body from upstairs – the dead man.

Back at the station, on checking information, the police knew that Exton Avenue had had its share of criminal goings-on! There had been the case of a Mrs Olsen who went shopping one day and had never been since. Then an invalid woman had been found strangled in a chest freezer and about the time of her death the same house had been burgled! And now the police had this new strange case to deal with!

And here is where this story takes a turn for the unexpected! Martha's head injury was to have near fatal results that would change her life forever. From the normal human being she had been, she became a creature of little understanding or memory who would be mentally scarred for life. Her injuries were so severe she would spend the rest of her days in a mental institution, at times locked away in a padded room for her own safety and that of those caring for her as she was often violent. Ironic – don't you think? – when the Jim she had cared for all those years had been in a similar situation, though maybe not so violent and he did appear to have moments of lucidity.

And what of Jim, you may ask? Jim's life was to take an even stranger turn! He had fallen down the stairs behind Martha and had sustained a head injury, cracking his head hard on the wall and stairs as he fell; but the outcome of this for Jim proved very different from what happened to Martha.

The Westminster clock in the hall chimed the hour at precisely 1 a.m., and Jim began to regain consciousness. He had ended up lying across Martha's back at the bottom of the stairs. As he came round he gradually raised himself into a sitting position. He turned Martha over a little, but she was unconscious. At first he thought she was dead! Memories began to come back to Jim of things he hadn't remembered or understood for years, and many things began to make sense to him. It was as if his mind had opened up again. He was regaining his senses after all these years. He even had the presence of mind to check for a pulse in Martha's neck, and the weak response he got told him she was still alive.

He began to wonder what to do for the best. There had opened up a chance of freedom for him now. He felt he could recover well enough and make plans to make up for all the years he'd missed out on. Yes, that's what he'd do. But how? If he 'disappeared', he might make a new life for himself. He'd get a new identity. It was a miracle that he could think so clearly now – a miracle fall, that's what it was, he told himself! He was becoming more coherent and clear in his head by the minute, and almost in complete control of himself. But one thing did not change: he still harboured strong feelings against Martha. He blamed her for his 'lost' years and determined to avenge himself. He had suffered, and now it would be her turn! He didn't know how he would achieve this, but achieve it he would.

They do say a serious fall and head injury (which Jim suffered) can sometimes reverse a mental condition, even if the brain is injured, and this is what seems to have happened in Jim's case. Doctors say it is very rare to make a recovery, but not impossible.

Jim had a plan, and this is what he did. He managed, with difficulty, to get himself upstairs to his room. He got a large suitcase out of the cupboard and started packing his belongings into it – clothes, papers, etc. He needed another bag. He packed the rest in a holdall. Then he checked he'd left nothing by which he could be traced. It was fortunate that only a few weeks earlier Martha had persuaded Jim to have a good clear-out of stuff he didn't need. That was helpful as he had little to take with him. Money – that's what he needed. He searched among Martha's belongings and helped himself to over £800 he found in a cash box. He'd had to force the lock.

So here he was, packed and ready to leave the house where he had been a 'captive' for so long. At least, that was how Jim saw it. The money would see him right for a little while. He remembered that years ago he had deposited a large amount of cash in a safety- deposit box in a lock-up at a post office where he used to live. He still had the key, and he just hoped the money would still be there! He would have to travel quite a way to get it, he knew, but he'd sort that out later.

Next Jim went into the spare room to make sure Clive was dead, though Jim knew he must be. Still wearing his gloves, he pulled the knife from Clive's chest and made his way downstairs. Then he placed the knife carefully in Martha's hand, pressing her fingers round it. It would look as if Martha had stabbed Clive to death. There would be none of Jim's fingerprints on the knife as he had kept his gloves on throughout the evening.

The hall clock chimed the hour: 2 a.m. Time to go.

Jim called a taxi, which arrived after twenty minutes. Jim wore a hooded coat, which almost concealed his face. The taxi driver would not be able to identify Jim if the occasion arose – if the police ever got that far. Surely it would not be long before the whole horrible murder would be discovered. Jim was determined to cover every eventuality so he would never be caught. Jim got in the taxi and asked the driver if he knew of a hotel in the town where he could stay for the night. Fifteen minutes later the driver stopped outside such a one and Jim paid him and went on into the building, where he booked a room. He would stay in this hotel – in his room, for the most part – until he decided what the next step would be.

On the second morning of his stay, Jim was glancing through the daily paper that was available to the hotel guests, and there it was: the headline 'Murder on Exton Avenue'. Underneath was written, 'Man found stabbed to death; woman unconscious with serious head injuries; police enquiries ongoing'.

"Terrible state of affairs, eh, mate?" a hotel cleaner remarked to Jim.

"Yes, shocking," Jim replied.

"You aren't safe in your own house these days, and that's a fact."

"You're right there," Jim said.

Chapter 52

Oh, so it looked like Martha was still alive. Jim decided to stay a few more days at the hotel. He'd have to decide what to do after that. It was in the next day's paper: more news of the murder! Jim read that the unconscious woman had been taken to hospital, to the psychiatric ward in the general hospital, where the police were waiting to question her.

All had become quite clear to Jim now since his fall. He'd found other things besides money in Martha's cash box. He'd found Martha's diaries – lots of them! She'd kept them religiously all through the years they'd been together. He read them over and over again in his hotel room, and what he'd been unaware of for so many years began to be clear to him now. He had over ten years to catch up on!

But the police? There was the problem. There would be enquiries and . . . Oh he'd sort things out somehow.

Meanwhile he'd begun to feel such a power within himself he was sure he could do anything now he set out to do. Yes, things were going to change in all sorts of ways from now on, he'd see to that.

Now Jim knew where Martha was! He would visit the hospital to see what sort of shape she was in, but he'd need to convince the staff there he had the right to see her. He knew there would be tight security there.

He reached the hospital and was directed to the psychiatric wing. In the waiting area there were several visitors seated. Jim joined them. He watched the comings and goings of staff and visitors. He must have been sitting there for over half an hour when he noticed three members of staff (probably doctors, he thought) go through a door which showed 'Staff Only'. They were wearing white coats with their name labels on the pockets. After about five minutes they reappeared wearing their 'civvies' and looked as if they were going home off duty.

Jim got up and, giving the appearance of reading a noticeboard near the 'Staff Only' door, he tentatively moved nearer this door. He took his chance and went in. He couldn't see anyone about. Three white coats were hanging up near the door. Jim removed one of them and put it on. The label tag read 'Dr Angelis Student Assessor'.

So that was to be Jim's title for the present. It did occur to him he might look a bit too old for a student, but he could be taken for a late developer looking for a change of occupation! In his new disguise he was sure he'd get to see Martha. Jim had overheard the real Dr Angelis remark to his colleagues, "Well, that's the first day over; only twenty-three to go!" And they'd all laughed. Would this work? It was a daring plan, but Jim hoped so.

Next Jim went to the information board by the nurses' station. On it was a list of rooms and the name of the patient in each room. One stood out: 'Martha Gibson Room 10 Level 2'.

Jim made his way there. A nurse was sitting writing at a desk outside Room 10. She looked up and seeing Jim with his label on his pocket she pressed the combination-lock numbers and the door opened to let Jim in to see Martha!

As he entered the room the nurse told Jim, "You won't get much sense out of this lady, Dr Angelis, I'm afraid."

Jim took a few steps into the room. He saw that Martha was in a wheelchair with her back towards him. Esther had once been in a wheelchair like that, but Martha could remember nothing of that now – not in the state she was in.

"Hello, Martha. I am Dr Angelis."

Martha made no sign of recognising that it was Jim who spoke to her.

Just then the nurse came in and said, "Excuse me, Doctor, but these flowers have just been left at the front desk. Someone left them for this lady, Martha. There was no name to say who sent them; they are just to be given to Martha Gibson here, Doctor."

Jim, alias Dr Angelis, took the violets and raised them so that Martha could smell their scent. She began to tremble uncontrollably and made a moaning noise, which after a few seconds turned to a high-pitched scream! She appeared to have little movement in her limbs, but with a tremendous effort she knocked the violets out of Jim's hand and on to the floor. She tried to raise herself a little out of the wheelchair, but couldn't. The violent screams brought in two other nurses very quickly, and they tried to calm her. She would not be calmed and resisted the nurses with the little might she had. An injection by the first nurse quickly put an end to the struggle and Martha flopped sideways over the wheelchair, stilled! Two of the nurses wheeled her out of the room.

"Well, you've seen for yourself, Dr Angelis, how this patient acts and how her condition affects her. One minute she's as calm as can be, but at other times she becomes very agitated, just mumbling and moaning to herself incoherently. We've many more tests to do to see how we can help her, but our head psychiatrist doesn't hold out much hope. He is sure she can never be cured. She is another patient we know will be in here for life."

Jim nodded, thanked the nurse and said he had two more patients to observe on Level 1. He took the lift downstairs and went into the men's toilets. He left the white coat in a cubicle there and proceeded to leave the hospital, walking out of Martha's life!

"Move along there! Make way for the ambulance, please," said a policeman to a crowd of onlookers outside the hospital.

There had evidently been an accident in the road outside the hospital entrance. A body was lifted gently from under a lorry and wrapped up completely in a blanket, head and all, then placed in an ambulance. At least it hadn't far to travel!

Two women standing by were discussing the incident.

"Walked straight out in the middle of the road, 'e did – never looked nowhere. I seed 'im with me own eyes. The poor lorry driver didn't stand a chance!" said the first woman.

"Never!" said the second woman. "Didn't see nothin' meself. Come out of the 'ospital, you say? Was 'e a patient?"

"Could 'ave been," said the first woman. "I mean, they didn't oughta let patients out of there – well, not with 'em being mental an' all that. Stands to reason they ain't safe in the traffic. Anyway, 'e won't be a patient no more, poor soul, for 'e is surely a goner!"

"No more 'e will, an' that's a fact," said the second woman. "Ooh, just look at them beautiful flowers you've got there today, love – beautiful colours, eh? I expect you does a good trade 'ere with the 'ospital visitors an' all. Good place to 'ave a stall, I should say. Wish I could afford them posh roses," said the second woman.

"P'raps yer old man'll give yer a bunch for yer birthday, love," laughed the stallholder.

"Some 'opes dearie – bunch 'o fives, more like!" cackled the second woman.

"'Ere, 'ave these, love – cheer yer up," said the stallholder.

"Ooh, thanks, dearie. Violets – 'ow pretty! I ain't 'ad none o' them for years! Thanks very much."

"Yer welcome, love."

"Well, must be on me way. Got to get me old man's dinner on. Bye, dearie."

"Bye, love," said the flower seller.

***

Perhaps James Maddox's coffin with its brass nameplate will come in useful after all. Just a thought!

THE END.

www.ingramcontent.com/pod-product-compliance
Lightning Source LLC
Chambersburg PA
CBHW020842260626
47169CB00003B/1098